game? Will a person who creates games that no one has ever imagined before suddenly appear?

No matter how much I think about it, I never come to an answer. Perhaps the boundaries of my world will never be widened by a game again.

But, fortunately, I have novels. There are limits to what someone like me can write, and due to my lack of ability and experience, nothing I write turns out as I'd like, and I fumble to take even a half-step, let alone a full one, forward.

When I try to write a certain novel, I always lose my nerve. Am I capable of writing it? Is it too much for me?

Even so, I continue to write, somehow, and in that time, I'm simply desperate. When I look back once I finish writing, there's a path behind me. Then, I'm able to see I've walked all this way.

I've run out of pages.

To my editor, K, to Eiri Shirai-san, to the designers of KOME-WORKS, among others, to everyone involved in production and sales of this book, and finally, to all of you people now holding this book, I offer my heartfelt appreciation and all of my love. Now, I lay down my pen for today. I hope we will meet again.

Ao Jyumonji

Occasionally, I wonder what the ideal game is to me. I've played a lot of RPGs. So, is it a game of that type, perhaps?

The ones that left a strong impression on me are *Dragon Quest III* and *V, Final Fantasy II, IV,* and *VII,* as well as *Romancing SaGa,* and also the MMORPGs *Ultima Online* and *EverQuest,* I suppose. RPGs of the same type as the ones I just listed or types that developed from them are still being produced today, but it feels like rather than following a path of evolving, they're following one of growing depth, or perhaps of division into narrow subcategories.

Furthermore, when it comes to MMORPGs, *World of Warcraft* swept the globe, and with later games finding ways to compensate for its weaknesses and refine the formula, it feels to me like it's been nearly perfected, and we're seeing the limits of what can be done.

When I first touched *Dragon Quest, Final Fantasy,* and the early MMORPGS, I was struck with the feeling that a new world was expanding before my eyes. My own small, narrow world was instantly expanded, and I set foot into it. Everything I saw and heard was new, and I didn't want to leave. As a matter of fact, there was a period where I shut myself away in there.

What kind of game would have to appear to make me feel as I did back then? Is that something that can be brought about by the advance of technology? Or can existing elements be combined to create a new type of

# Grimgar

*of*

# Fantasy

*and*

# Ash

# Grimgar of Fantasy and Ash

## level. 2 – Everything is Precious

Presented by Ao Jyumonji Illustrated by Eiri Shirai

"I see. Well, if we were to go somewhere else, where would be good?"

It was almost like she already had her answer prepared.

"The Cyrene Mines," Merry answered briefly and immediately. Haruhiro almost said, **But isn't that where?** But he bit back the words.

"SURE!"

*Haruhiro could hear his response. But there was no sign of him climbing up. Not Ranta.*
*Rather than Ranta, a kobold started climbing up the rope ladder.*
*Moguzo kicked it down, but another kobold came up after it.*

## "The Story So Far"

### "Awaken."

On hearing that word, Haruhiro awakens to find himself in the unfamiliar world of Grimgar.

In order to survive, Haruhiro forms a party with others who find themselves in similar circumstances, Manato, Ranta, Yume, Shihoru and Moguzo, and together they end up living the lives of a group of volunteer soldiers just getting their start.

However, while Renji and his group, who arrived at the same time, are getting ahead of them, Haruhiro and the others struggle even against supposedly weak enemies like goblins. Then, just as things look like they're finally getting on track, they lose Manato, the central figure of the party.

With no time to wallow in despair, out of necessity
Haruhiro and the others add a new priest, Merry, to their party.
Goblins aren't the only enemies they face.
They also battle with their own lack of power.
As well as Merry's past.

As the party face a reality that just won't go their way, they grow stronger little by little until finally Haruhiro and the others succeed in avenging Manato.

However, the adventure isn't over yet...

# Grimgar of Fantasy and Ash

### level. 2 — Everything is Precious

**Presented by**
## AO JYUMONJI

*Illustrated by*
## EIRI SHIRAI

GRIMGAR OF FANTASY AND ASH, LEVEL. 2

© 2013 Ao Jyumonji
Illustrations by Eiri Shirai

First published in Japan in 2013 by
OVERLAP Inc., Ltd., Tokyo.
English translation rights arranged with
OVERLAP Inc., Ltd., Tokyo.

Seven Seas books may be purchased in bulk for promotional,
educational, or business use. Please contact your local
bookseller or the Macmillan Corporate and Premium Sales
Department at 1-800-221-7945, extension 5442, or by
e-mail at MacmillanSpecialMarkets@macmillan.com.

Seven Seas and the Seven Seas logo are trademarks of
Seven Seas Entertainment, LLC. All rights reserved.

Follow Seven Seas Entertainment online at gomanga.com.
Experience J-Novel Club books online at j-novel.club.

Translation: Sean McCann
J-Novel Editor: Emily Sorensen
Book Layout: Karis Page
Cover Design: Nicky Lim
Copy Editor: Tom Speelman
Proofreader: John Sullivan
Light Novel Editor: Jenn Grunigen
Production Assistant: CK Russell
Production Manager: Lissa Pattillo
Editor-in-Chief: Adam Arnold
Publisher: Jason DeAngelis

ISBN: 978-1-626926-60-8
Printed in Canada
First Printing: August 2017
10 9 8 7 6 5 4 3 2 1

# [ TABLE OF CONTENTS ]

# Characters

## YUME

Airheaded soothing-type. Speaks an iffy sort of Kansai dialect?

Class: Hunter

## HARUHIRO

Sleepy eyes. Passive-type. Provisional leader.

Class: Thief

## SHIHORU

Shy and withdrawn. Hard worker with little presence.

Class: Mage

## RANTA

Selfish, flaky joker. #1 most unpopular.

Class: Dread Knight

## MERRY

Cool beauty. Has more experience as a volunteer soldier and is a little more of an adult.

Class: Priest

## MOGUZO

Bear-type. A somewhat slow, but reliable bear.

Class: Warrior

## Team Renji

**Ron** — Class: Paladin — The Team's No. 2.
**Sassa** — Class: Thief — Flashy woman. Probably an M.
**Adachi** — Class: Mage — Wears glasses.
**Chibi** — Class: Priest — Mascot.

## Day Breakers

**Kemuri** — Class: Paladin
**Pingo** — Class: Necromancer
**Shima** — Class: Sword Dancer
**Lilia** — Class: Shaman

## Other

**Kikkawa** — Class: Warrior
**Hayashi** — Class: Warrior
**Michiki** — Class: Warrior
**Mutsumi** — Class: Mage
**Ogu** — Class: Thief

## Other Characters

*RENJI*
Class: Warrior

Head of Team Renji.
Wild beast-type. Dangerous.

*MANATO*
Class: Priest

Kept the party together.
Was a good guy. (Past tense)

*SOMA*
Class: Samurai

Started the Day Breakers Clan.
Seems to have some objective.

## [ OLD CITY OF DAMURO ]

Damuro, roughly 4 km northwest of Alterna, was once the Arabakia Kingdom's second largest city. However, it fell to an attack by the Undying Empire and became a town of the undead. Amidst the chaos following the death of No-Life King, the goblins that were being treated like slaves staged a rebellion. The battle between the undead and goblins over Damuro lasted for a long time; in that time, the Arabakia Kingdom moved forward with the construction of Alterna. The goblins built a kingdom based out of Damuro which has never attacked Alterna. Cautious of the human race's strength of arms, the goblins seem afraid of entering an all-out war with them. The southeast section of Damuro, the Old City, is half-ruined and now primarily inhabited by lower class goblins. They are perfect targets for fresh volunteer soldiers to build real battle experience. However, some ambitious goblins among them are amassing power in the Old City to make a name for themselves in the New City, so it is important not to get careless. A goblin that has hobgoblins following it around is especially dangerous.

## [ DEADHEAD WATCHING KEEP ]

Roughly 6 km north of Alterna. Garrisoned by orcs, it is an imposing fortress with towers at its center. There have been many times in the past where orc forces have massed at this keep for an assault on Alterna, but thus far, they have always been driven off. It has fallen to attacks by the Alterna Frontier Army numerous times, but is always retaken. It would be an ideal target for a group of volunteer soldiers that have trained themselves up a bit.

## [ CYRENE MINES ]

8 km northwest of Alterna. These mines were once managed by the Arabakia Kingdom, but are now occupied by kobolds and have developed a unique ecology. The mines are stratified into levels—more than ten of them, it has been said. The highest levels have the weakest kobolds, with the level of danger increasing the deeper you go. The first and second levels are inhabited by lower class kobolds and are not very dangerous, but caution becomes necessary from the third level down. Merry once faced a particularly vicious kobold on the fifth level with her comrades, Hayashi, Michiki, Mutsumi, and Ogu. She lost three comrades in that battle.

## [ MONSTERS ]

### KOBOLDS

A humanoid race with doglike heads. Built somewhat smaller than humans, they stand about 150cm tall. However, some large individuals can reach 170cm. Not as intelligent as humans, like the dogs they resemble, they have a well-defined hierarchy and have built a society with a rigid class structure. They have strong bonds within their race, but are hostile to outsiders. Preferring to live in burrows, they are skilled with their hands, though not to the same degree as dwarfs or gnomes. They have developed a level of metallurgy technology that is not to be underestimated. Due to their occult beliefs, all kobolds carry talismans. The complexity of these talismans rises in proportion to the owner's class, and these can sell for a lot of money. Volunteer soldiers have names for the different classes, such as lesser kobolds or elder kobolds, and use them to distinguish different individuals.

**ON KOBOLD VARIETIES**

● **Lesser Kobolds:**
- Appear on the first level and in the vicinity of the mines. Have weak bodies and equipment.

● **Kobolds:**
- Low Workers: Inhabit the second layer.
- Workers: Inhabit the third layer and lower. Also known as followers.

● **Elder Kobolds:**
- Foremen: Inhabit the third level and beneath. Direct the other kobolds. Bring followers around with them.

*Note: In addition to these, there are kobolds with fixed roles within each class.*

## ORCS ...........................................................................

A green skinned and—from a human perspective—hideous race. They have flat noses, pointy ears, big mouths, and tusks. Built slightly larger than humans, not so much in terms of height, but in terms of bulk. They have the tendency to dye their hair in a variety of colors; those who wish to stand out and appear strong tend to dye their hair in vibrant hues. They also like to dress up. Their intelligence is by no means low and, while a little rough, they are not so different from humans. However, they are bellicose, and even within their own race, their conflicts are unending. These often result in bloodshed. Their level of civilization is not much different from that of humans, and they wear a wide variety of items. Due to the difference in body size, it is quite difficult for humans to use orcish items as is, but not completely impossible. In many cases, they can be modified to allow them to be used. Like with humans, their possessions can vary considerably, but loot taken from them often sells for a good amount of money. Also, orc society uses a currency resembling buttons made out of crystal. Depending on their size, these may sell for anywhere from five to five hundred copper. Since the times of the Alliance of Kings, orcs have been viewed as a race equal to the undead, and with No-Life King now gone, they could be said to be the most prosperous race in the frontier. To humans, they are a powerful enemy—perhaps even their natural enemy. The occasional attacks on Alterna are nearly always carried out by orcs. Some orcs can even speak the human language.

Grimgar
*of*
Fantasy *and* Ash

# 1. No Comparison

The party had sold off their loot for the day, split the profits, and were in the middle of idly chatting about what to do next.

Dong, dong, dong, dong, dong, dong!

The sound of bells rang wildly through Alterna's marketplace.

"Oh, it's six," Haruhiro furrowed his brow. "...No, that's not it, right? I mean, there were seven bells the last time they rang. Besides, the bell for 6:00 PM doesn't ring so frantically—"

"What, what, what?!" Ranta shook his curly-haired head left and right to look around.

"Hmm." Yume pulled on her braids, her eyes going wide. "Wonder what it is."

"An emergency...I guess?" Shihoru nestled closer to Yume.

Moguzo rubbed the back of his helmet, looking about worriedly. "...Muh?"

"No, it can't be..." Merry lowered her posture a little, squinting her eyes. "An enemy raid?"

"Huh?" Haruhiro cocked his head to the side. He knew what the word meant, but he wasn't used to hearing it. "By an enemy raid, you mean—"

*Wahhhh!* A cry rang out.

*Where was that from? It sounded far away,* Haruhiro thought.

Ranta flared his nostrils, shouting, "Hey, hey, hey, hey!" and "Oh, oh, oh!"

*What're you so excited about? Are you an idiot?*

"Merry, what enemies?" Haruhiro shouted, to which Merry quickly responded, "Probably orcs."

*Orcs?*

"Run!" someone screamed.

"Orcs!"

"It's orcs!"

"Orcs!"

"The orcs are here!"

"They're invading...!"

"Huh?" Yume brought her index finger to her chin. "Is Ochre-kun someone's friend?"

"That's clearly not it!" Haruhiro reflexively corrected her.

That was when it happened.

The people who had been going about their business in the market turned into a raging stream. It only took an instant. Haruhiro was caught in the wave of people. Now, he could only go wherever he was being pushed.

"Wai—" Ranta tried to resist it, but his efforts were in vain. "What is this?!"

"Uwahwahh!" Moguzo's eyes were spinning. Because his body was so big, he was getting elbowed and kicked a lot. It looked unpleasant.

"M-my hat...!" Shihoru's hat fell off.

Haruhiro said "Oh!" and reached out, managing to catch Shihoru's hat—

But with the mass of people pushing against him, he was pulled away from the rest of his comrades.

"Haru-kun!" He heard Yume's voice.

"Haru...?!"

*Was that voice Merry's? I can still just barely make out Moguzo's head. But there's no way I can get over there.*

"G-guys...!" Haruhiro desperately stretched out his hand. *It's no use. I don't even know where Moguzo is anymore.* "Everyone, be careful...!"

*Really, the one who needs to be careful is me! If I fight against the flow, I'll be pushed down. I'll be knocked to the ground, trampled, and killed. I don't want that. For now, I'll have to go with the flow.*

"It's an enemy raid," Merry had said. *An enemy? What are orcs...? Orcs.*

*I feel like I've heard of them, or maybe I haven't. Either way, something unusual is happening. If this is an enemy raid, that means enemies have come to attack, right? Alterna's under attack by these orc things, right? Still, if we're running away, where do we run to?*

*This is a town. Everyone lives here. Alterna is surrounded by high, thick walls. There's nowhere safer than this. —Or there shouldn't be. I think. Probably. But that safe place is being attacked. Does that mean, maybe, we're in serious trouble...?*

Stalls were being flipped over. Goods were being scattered around and trampled.

*What a waste.* There were even carts that had been knocked over, with their frames broken.

*The owner must be in shock. No, that's the least of my worries right now.*

"Gyahhhhhhhhhhhh...!" came the scream from up ahead.

"They're here! The enemy...!"

"That way's no good!"

"Run, back the other way...!"

Immediately, the wave of people started surging back in the opposite direction. However, it was impossible to suddenly change course like that; those up front were trying to change direction, but the ones behind them were still trying to move forward. Worst of all, Haruhiro was caught in the middle, unable to move at all.

"Hey, that hurts, you know! Q-quit shoving...!"

*At this rate, I'm going to be crushed to death. That's how I'm going to die? That's not even funny.*

Haruhiro somehow managed to push people aside, making his way through the crowd. Up ahead, there was a cart with a dark-colored curtain over it that hadn't been destroyed, so he went inside.

"Urkh! It stinks..."

*It smells weird. It's more than just the smell, though. The stuff displayed on the shelves is weird to begin with. Dead animals? Stuffed and preserved? Then there are bones, teeth, and feathers. And...accessories? Assembled from those things.*

"Come this way."

There was a sudden voice, and Haruhiro jumped with a start. When he looked, there was an old lady in blackish clothes deep inside the cart. She looked extremely shady. While he stood there indecisively, the old lady shouted "Hurry!" at him. Haruhiro hesitantly headed to the back of the cart.

"...Um, is this your store, granny?" he asked.

"Granny, is it? What a rude young boy. Call me Lady."

"L-Lady," Haruhiro corrected himself, and the old woman grinned.

"...Set, go," she finished for him.

"...I said Lady, not ready."

"Your comeback wasn't snappy enough."

*Your setup was weak to begin with! What's with this old hag?* Haruhiro thought, but he refrained from saying anything.

The old woman shrugged as if to say, *Good grief.* "I am Baba."

"Which is exactly what you are, since it means 'an old woman.'"

"*Hmph.* That was better than your last attempt, at least."

"Well, thanks..."

"Work at it. Anyway, once again, I am Baba. Baba the Magician. As you can see, this shop sells goods for use in magic. Are you a volunteer soldier?"

"Well, yes." While being careful not to breathe through his nose, Haruhiro looked towards the outside. Since the cart was covered with a curtain, he couldn't see what was happening, but there was still a lot of noise, so the incident was probably still ongoing.

"...Is this an incident? I guess it is," he said.

"The orcs, you mean? Well, this happens once in a *loooong* while. Hm? Are you a rookie, then?"

"Well, I haven't been at it long. Volunteer soldiering, that is."

"The way you're acting, you must be a virgin."

"Vir...?!"

"You idiot. I don't mean whether you've slept with a woman or not. A volunteer soldier isn't a real man until he's killed an orc. We treat those who haven't experienced that yet like virgins. What, are you a double virgin then?"

"...Single, double, triple, whatever, I don't care!"

"You lack ambition!" Baba thrust a finger in Haruhiro's direction. "You're a man, aren't you? You're young! You want to sleep with women, you want to kill orcs! What are you holding back your desires for?!"

"It feels like more trouble than it's worth."

"You moron!" Baba spewed spittle and seemed ready to keep going when—*swish!* The curtain was drawn back.

"Ah..." Haruhiro blinked.

*Someone's here. Someone—no, something? It's not...a person.*

*I mean, it's got green skin.*

*Its body is big. More broad than tall. It's incredibly thick.*

*It has a smushed nose, pointy ears, and a wide mouth with boar-like tusks.*

*Its hair is bright red.*

*It's in armor and carrying a heavy-looking sword with a single-edged blade.*

*What is this guy?*

"It's an orc," Baba croaked, pulling out some sort of rod. "To think it would enter the shop! V-volunteer soldier, take care of it! It's time to make a man of yourself!"

"Huh? M-me?!" Haruhiro went to draw his dagger, but was too anxious to try anything with it. "I-I can't do it, not alone! I'm a thief!"

"Well, *I'm* just an old hag! Go on, buck up, thief!" Baba gave Haruhiro a good hard shove in the back.

For calling herself an old hag, she was pretty strong. Haruhiro stumbled towards the orc with a "Whoa, whoa, whoa," almost tripping.

The orc shouted something at him in a language with a lot of *shu's*, *sha's*, *bah's*, and *oh's*, then stabbed its sword at him.

"No, no, no...?!" Haruhiro dodged.

Somehow, he got out of the way, but fell onto one of the display stands, causing Baba to scold him with a "Come on, what do you think you're doing?!"

"Shouting at me isn't helping right now...!" Haruhiro rolled on top of the display to escape.

The orc clambered up onto the display stand, chasing after him. "Ohshubaguda!"

*It's no good. I'm dead. I'm seriously gonna die!* Haruhiro screamed, throwing anything that came to hand at it. Even when he hit, the orc didn't care. *Oh, crap! Oh, crap! Oh, crap! This isn't good.* Haruhiro dived through the curtain, heading outside the cart.

"...Huh? It's not coming?"

As he was thinking that...

"H-hey now, volunteer soldier!" he heard Baba's voice. "Are you going to abandon this poor old woman? You monster...!"

"It's easy to say that, but..."

In the distance, he saw another orc. It was a large enough force to call this an enemy raid, so it shouldn't have been a surprise, but there was more than one orc.

*There's a bunch of them. Not good.*

*This is bad. Real bad.*

*I should run. Find somewhere to hide until someone comes along and,* bam, *takes out all the orcs. I don't care about Baba. She's a total stranger to me. I don't owe her anything, and I doubt I could save her anyway.*

"I don't have any other choice...right?" he murmured, half-convinced, to himself.

Haruhiro took a deep breath. Then he pulled back the curtain on Baba's cart. "Dammit...!"

*Why? What are you doing? Weren't you going to run away? No, I'd love to run away, but even if she's a total stranger, I'd have a hard time sleeping if I abandoned her. So, this is the only option. I really don't feel good about this, but, as a person, it's the only right thing to do.*

The orc swung its sword down. Baba blocked it with her staff, her face turning red as she groaned with exertion. Even though she was blocking it somehow—

*She's just barely holding in there. It's plain to see. Baba's crouching down. She's desperate. It's a damn good thing that staff is so sturdy. I guess I don't have time to be impressed by that, though.* Haruhiro drew his dagger and charged at the orc's back.

"Backstab...!"

The blade slid aside with a clang. It had armor which deflected the blow.

The orc turned around. "Gashuhah!" it cried.

"Volunteer soldier!" Baba's eyes were shining. "I think I might just fall in love!"

"Could you please not?! Seriously!" Haruhiro turned his back on the orcs. "F-follow me! Well, no, you don't have to...!"

Sadly for Haruhiro, the orc shifted focus from Baba to him.

*Yeah, I shouldn't have done this. I should've run for it after all. Too late for regrets now.*

The orc came after him, shouting, "Hahshu, hahshu, hahshu!"

Haruhiro got out of the cart and ran. As he was running, he

quickly ran out of breath. The orc was in heavy equipment, but it was fast. Haruhiro was lightly equipped and running as fast as he could. Even so, he couldn't pull away.

"Damn, you're scary...!"

Even while he complained, he tried running down narrow streets and forcing his way between carts to somehow shake the orc off his tail.

But the orc, with its clanking armor, continued to chase him everywhere he went.

*I'm about ready to give up. Um, excuse me. Can we just call this the finish line? You don't mind, right?*

*The finish line can be when I turn the next corner. I'll hang in until there. I probably can't handle any more than that. I'm at the end of my wits and stamina. I retire. I'm sorry.*

Haruhiro turned the corner, halfway ready to collapse.

"Get down!" a low, husky voice shouted at him.

Haruhiro did so and something flew over the top of his head.

*No, not something—a sword.*

Someone was around the corner—the owner of that husky voice— and that person had swung the sword.

The sword struck the orc head-on.

"Ogoh....!" it cried.

"...Huh?" Haruhiro turned around.

The orc's head had been lopped off. It was the silver-haired man with his back to him that had done it.

*Renji,* Haruhiro thought.

*He had become a volunteer soldier on the same day as Haruhiro. Or at least, I'm pretty sure he did,* Haruhiro thought, *even if it doesn't seem like it. On top of that cool-looking armor, he's wearing a fur-trimmed cape. The sword he's got looks sturdy and awesome, too. I knew he was different from the rest of us from the very beginning, but still, the gap between us is big. Huge. I mean, he did that in one blow?*

*With just one blow, he took down an orc.*

"You okay?" Renji asked, and Haruhiro nodded shakily.

*Wow. So lame. I'm pathetic. My face is burning with shame.*

Standing up in a hurry, he was about to at least say "Thank you" when someone shouted, "Renji, there's still more...!"

When Haruhiro looked, a man with a buzzcut wearing a fine suit of armor was pointing off into the distance.

*It's Ron. There are orcs coming from the direction he's pointing. More than one of them, too. There are two... No, three.*

"Zeel, mare, gram, fel, kanon," chanted Adachi the mage, a man wearing black-rimmed glasses, drawing elemental sigils with the tip of his staff.

*What kind of magic is that?* Haruhiro didn't know at all.

A blue elemental flew out, wrapping itself around one orc's leg. It tripped the orc up, and though it didn't fall over, the orc seemed to be having trouble walking.

However, even with their buddy slowed down, the other two orcs charged in like it didn't matter.

—Then, a long leg popped out of the alleyway, landing a flat-footed kick on one orc's knee.

The timing was perfect. There's no dodging that. It was probably the thief fighting skill Shatter.

The orc let out a "Gyaoh!" and stumbled.

*Who did that? That flashy outfit. That exposed skin. So sexy. Sassa, huh?*

"Well done!" Ron stepped forward and traded blows with an orc. Ron wasn't a small man, but the orc was amazingly well built. Even so, Ron seemed to be pushing it back.

"Hah, hah, hah, hah, hah...!"

However, the orc Sassa had hit with Shatter was steadying its feet through the pain and getting ready to aid its comrade.

In order to stop it, one girl rose up in the orc's way—

*Is what I would say, but she's way too tiny. She's got to be less than 150 cm. She's wearing priest's clothes and carrying what looks like a short staff, but she just looks like a kid playing dress-up. What on Earth does Chibi-chan plan to do?*

"No...!" Chibi held her staff out in front of her.

The orc shouted "Fah!" and swept the staff aside with its sword.

"Wha...?" Haruhiro lost his voice.

Rather than be knocked away, the staff traced an arc. Chibi-chan gave it a hefty spin. Using the momentum, she slammed the staff into the orc's lower body.

"Yah...!" she cried.

"Go, fuh...?!" the orc didn't collapse, but it stopped in its tracks.

Chibi-chan leapt back and Renji patted her on the head with his big hand.

"Nice work, Chibi," Renji said.

"Aw..." Chibi blushed deep red.

The next moment, Renji's sword bit into the orc's shoulder. Even though the orc wore sturdy armor, that apparently didn't matter against Renji.

Renji tore his sword free, planting a boot on the orc's chest and kicking it away.

As it spun away, the panicked orc was no longer a threat to Renji. He stabbed his sword through its throat and twisted.

"Ohhhhhhhhhhh...!" the orc moaned.

Ron attacked and attacked, finally forcing the other orc to take a knee. At this point, he'd won. Ron swung his sword down in a flurry of blows, splitting the orc's head open.

"There! Take that...!"

*...His strength is incredible. Also, man, is his voice loud.*

While Haruhiro stood there impressed by Ron's voice, Renji was closing in on the last orc, the one delayed by Adachi's magic.

Haruhiro watched admiringly.

*That stride. Barbara from the thieves' guild has a way of sliding her feet to run or walk without making noise. It's kinda like that.*

*That sword handling. It's a heavy-looking sword, but Renji swings it like it's his own arm.*

Renji cut through the orc's neck like it was made out of paper.

*No, you can't cut through it like that. Bones are hard. Or so I thought, but...he really did chop right through it, so that's a mystery.*

"That's one down," Ron patted himself on the shoulder with the flat of his blade.

Haruhiro stared in a daze. Though, perhaps thanks to that, he was able to notice it. Rather than focusing on a single point, he was looking at the whole scene when—

*Something moved. On top of the building. On the roof.*

Haruhiro shouted. "Renji, above you...!"

Renji instantly jumped aside. Had he hesitated, he'd have been cut down.

That guy jumped off the roof and came at Renji.

*It's an orc. Of course, it's an orc. Its hair is white. It's got a luster to it, so it could look silver, too. Coincidentally, Renji's hair is silver, too.*

*Is there a rule saying silver-haired guys have to be insane? Because that orc is clearly insane, too. Its body is big, and on top of wearing black armor, it's got this cape with a tiger stripe pattern that's probably real tiger fur, which is insanely flashy. Those tattoos all over its face are insane. Its yellow eyes look so wild, it's insane. Despite that, its expression is calm and it looks pretty smart, which is crazy.*

*And then there's the sword. The one-edged sword that orc has is purple-ish, long, thick, and sharp-looking with a jagged back side that looks bizarre.*

On top of that, when it turned back to face Renji, about ten more orcs showed themselves on top of the nearby buildings. The situation was hopelessly bad.

As the orcs were about to come down from the roof, the boss in the tiger cape raised his left hand to stop them. Then, it said, "Me."

—*Huh? "Me"...?*

"Me Ish Dogran. What your name."

*It spoke. Broken or not, that orc spoke human language.*

Renji's lips loosened a little. Apparently, he was smiling.

*I'm amazed he can smile. In a situation like this, isn't that weird? It's weird, right?*

"It's Renji. You want to fight me, Ish Dogran?"

"Ongashurahdu!" When the orc boss—apparently named Ish Dogran—raised his voice, the other orcs lowered their weapons.

*Is he declaring a one-on-one battle, maybe?*

"Don't any of you interfere," Renji said to his comrades in a low voice.

*You're doing this? You're really doing this? You're serious? Apparently, you are.*

*Or, rather, they're already going at it.*

*Which of them swung first?* Haruhiro couldn't tell.

There was a clatter of metal on metal as their blades collided. Sparks flew.

Their blades locked. They pushed back and forth.

That wasn't all; with slight changes in position, they slammed their hips into each other. If Haruhiro took a hip thrust like that, he'd fall over in one shot. They were trying to unbalance one another, but neither fell.

They leapt apart.

Ish Dogran aimed for Renji's legs. Renji leapt out of the way, slashing at Ish Dogran's head.

Ish Dogran deflected it with his forearm guard, taking a deep breath—

*His cape.*

He threw the tiger cape at Renji. Haruhiro was caught completely by surprise, but not Renji. Without haste or panic, he grabbed the cape and stabbed at Ish Dogran with his sword.

Ish Dogran had probably hoped to startle Renji with the cape, creating an opening to attack. That plan failed, so he backed away. He backed away, falling into a fighting stance.

"Good. Human. You good warrior."

"Oh, yeah?" Renji responded shortly as he closed in on Ish Dogran.

They exchanged blows again. However, this time, Renji was on the attack.

Haruhiro unconsciously tightened his hands into fists. *You can do it. You can beat him. Go. Go get him. Do it! Take him down...!*

It looked like Renji had the advantage, and he should have. But suddenly, Ish Dogran's sword cut deeply into his left arm.

*Why...? I don't get it.* Haruhiro didn't understand at all.

Renji put some distance between them, shaking his left arm. He had a pretty bad wound near his elbow, and it was bleeding profusely. Renji's comrades all either shouted out or gulped, while the orcs gave a cheer.

Renji let his left arm slump to his side.

*Looks like he plans to use his sword with just his right. Well, with that wound, he doesn't have much choice. Renji's sword's huge. He's at a disadvantage now.*

Despite that, Renji took a deep breath and smiled.

"Not bad," he smirked. This smile was different from the last one. He didn't just loosen his lips, he grinned with his whole face.

Haruhiro shuddered. He honestly thought Renji was frightening. *Renji's scary. Well, he's always been scary.*

Renji went on the attack again. Ish Dogran turned his blade aside.

*Ish Dogran's wielding with two hands, while Renji only has one. Renji's slashes are always going to be lighter. He can't win this with a straight up exchange of blows.*

In fact, Renji's sword looked like it was going to be sent flying and, though he managed to hold on to it somehow, he was left wide open from his face to his chest.

*This is bad.*

"Eek...!" Chibi screamed.

Ish Dogran slammed the back of his fist into Renji's face.

*He's not bare-handed. Ish Dogran's forearm guards are probably metal, and they cover his fists, too.* There was blood everywhere in an instant; Renji's nose was broken and smashed.

Even so, Renji was still smiling. He attacked again. It was deflected, his blow knocked away, and he suffered a counterattack.

As they watched, Renji became covered in wounds all over. He was wearing armor, but not the type that protected him everywhere. There were several gaps in it which Ish Dogran's attacks precisely targeted. On top of that, with his wicked sword, the orc could cleave through a little armor.

"Ohshu! Ohshu! Ohshu!" the orcs stamped and cheered loudly.

*Renji's continuing his attack, but it's painful to watch. Stubbornness is all that's keeping him going at this point. That, and if he goes on the defensive, he'll be taken out immediately, so he has to keep attacking, or something like that.*

"Ron!" Haruhiro couldn't take it anymore. "Are you okay with not helping Renji? Adachi! Chibi-chan! Sassa! Renji's gonna die!"

"If we did that," Sassa said, looking pale, "Renji would kill us later." Even as she sweated, she forced a mocking laugh.

"Uwah...!" Chibi-chan said with an incredible look on her face. Like she was trying to tell him something telepathically.

*I don't think it was a signal, though.*

Renji attacked and Ish Dogran turned his blade aside. The scene looked similar to what had happened a little earlier. Renji's sword was almost sent flying, but he somehow held on. But his face and chest were left wide open.

*This is bad. It's the same as last time. He's gonna die.*

Ish Dogran tried to punch Renji in the face. Renji didn't let him.

*He's wielding with both hands.* Renji suddenly switched to a two-handed grip and swung upwards. Ish Dogran leaned back and avoided it—

*But, that shouldn't be possible. Wasn't his left hand unusable? Still, Renji is holding his sword tightly with both hands right now.*

"Ahhhhhhhhhhhhhhhhhhhhhhhhhhhhhhhhhhhhhhhhh...!" Renji roared like a bloodthirsty beast.

It was doubtful that it had made Ish Dogran falter, but the orc did pause for a moment.

Renji's sword swung down crosswise, burying itself in Ish Dogran's shoulder.

In the next moment, Renji let go of his sword.

He pushed Ish Dogran down and punched him. He punched again, not even pausing for a breath. He punched him systematically, meticulously.

Ish Dogran moved no more.

The area fell silent, with only the dull sound of Renji punching Ish Dogran. His body was the only thing moving.

Finally, Renji clasped his hands together and raised them high. Then he slammed them down on Ish Dogran's head. Then, with a deep sigh, he snapped his head back and forth.

"You weren't bad. Ish Dogran. I'll remember your name."

Ron snorted. "You're a mess."

Adachi's eyes flashed, and he was glaring at the orcs on top of the building.

Sassa looked ready to collapse at any moment. Chibi-chan was rushing over to Renji's side.

Renji pushed Chibi-chan aside, picking up Ish Dogran's sword

and pointing it at the orcs.

"What're you gonna do now? If you want a fight, all of you come at me at once. I'll take you on."

*No—isn't that bluffing a little hard...?* Haruhiro couldn't help but feel that way. He was sure they were going to die, but in a situation like this, maybe you had to bluff big.

One orc waved an arm. Several orcs growled in protest, but when the orc who waved looked at them, they fell silent.

The orcs all retreated at once.

"We..." Haruhiro was ready to collapse on the spot. "We... survived?"

All of that had unfolded before his eyes, but still he couldn't believe it. Haruhiro looked at Renji. He looked at him again and again.

*Renji's really amazing. He's strong. It's stupid to try to compare the two of us and then act jealous or servile because of it... Renji's insane.*

*Totally insane.*

"Ah," Haruhiro looked down to his own hands. Then, he looked around. It was gone.

*Shihoru's mage hat was gone. When was I last holding it? There was too much other stuff going on, so I don't remember. Anyway, it looks like I've lost it.*

"What's wrong with me...?" he sighed.

Grimgar
of
Fantasy and Ash

## 2. Wishy-Washy Chairman

"—And that's how it went!" When he was sitting in a corner in Sherry's Tavern telling the story to his comrades like this, the excitement never stopped.

In fact, at some point, he realized that not only Ranta, Moguzo, Yume, Shihoru and Merry were listening to him, the people drinking at nearby tables were as well, and he became a little embarrassed.

Haruhiro cleared his throat.

"...Anyway, they were just amazing! Renji's party, that is. Actually, just Renji alone was amazing, really. That orc, Ish Dogran, was pretty tough, too, I think. Well, until halfway through, it was looking to me like Renji was going to get killed, after all. Oh, but, it was never actually like that at all, you know. He just sort of made it seem that way? You could say he was tricking us all, I guess? I mean, I was convinced Renji couldn't use his left arm. Ish Dogran looked like he totally believed it, too."

"Whoa!" Ranta messed up his curly hair. "Basically, he turned a bad situation into his trump card, and saved it for when things got even worse! Damn, that's so ballsy, I can't believe it! Damn, damn, damn! I wanna do that, too! I'll do it, I swear! 100%, I'm gonna do it!"

Yume looked coldly at Ranta. "Yeah, you go right ahead. If you fail, well, them's the breaks, right?"

"Like I'd fail! I'll obviously succeed! I guarantee it'll be a huge success!"

Shihoru—who, in the end, had been forced to buy a brand new mage hat—looked at him with exasperation. "...What basis do you have for that...?"

"Huh? Basis? Well, you know, uh..." Ranta thought deeply, but apparently drew a blank. "You moron, I don't need no stinking basis! Confidence is all I need! The confidence to say, yes, I can! You've *gotta* have that!"

Merry lifted her porcelain mug to her mouth, then took a short breath. "I definitely think confidence is important."

"I know, right?! That's Merry for you! She gets it. Because she's had a longer career than any of you guys! She's different! She's not like you small fry!"

Merry gave Ranta a silent but heavy look. "Overconfidence kills."

"Urkh..." It seemed Ranta had no comeback for that.

Of course not, because Merry's words had the ring of truth to them. After all, because her initial party had let an early taste of success go to their heads (to put it a little uncharitably), they'd suffered horribly for it. Merry had lost three comrades.

"B-but..." Moguzo mumbled. As much as he loved his helmet, he'd left it on the table. "Th-they're amazing. Really. Renji and his team, I mean. Even though they started at the same time as us, they've gotten pretty far ahead..."

Once Haruhiro finished regaling them with "The Legend of Renji," some of the customers near the table came over with grins on their faces, patting him on the shoulder and saying things like "You work hard now, Goblin Slayer," then they left.

Ranta clicked his tongue. "...Dammit, those jerks. They're making fun of us!"

"Now, now." Yume had her elbows on the table and was resting her face on her palms. "Yume thinks Yume and everyone should just go about doin' things at their own peace."

"That's pace, not peace," Haruhiro corrected her quickly, then nodded. "Yeah. I agree with Yume, I think. I mean, once I saw him in action...I couldn't help but think, 'Ah, he's just made of different stuff than we are.' We couldn't imitate him even if we tried, and, to be blunt, he's not even a useful reference for us..."

"...If we're reckless..." Shihoru looked down, frowning as if holding something back.

She might be remembering...him. The precious comrade Haruhiro and the others had lost.

"...If something we just can't ever fix happens, it'd all be for nothing..." she murmured.

"You're aiming too low!" Ranta pointed at Yume, then Haruhiro and then Shihoru, one after the other. "Just what kind of chickens are you people?! Most of the time, returns come with risks, got it?! No risk is no return and no point! Low risk is low return, and if you want a high return, you've gotta be prepared to take the high risks!"

Haruhiro got a bit miffed by that. "Doing things in a way that minimizes the risk and maximizes the return should be perfectly valid. In fact, we've been doing reasonably well that way."

"'Reasonably,' huh," Ranta scoffed. "I'll just come out and say it. The only thing we've been doing a 'reasonable' job of is circling the drain. Do you get that? Do ya? Buddy, look around a bit."

"Huh? Look around...?" Haruhiro looked around Sherry's Tavern.

Now that Ranta mentioned it, Haruhiro noticed that out of all the volunteer soldiers here, he and his party were far and away the most shabby looking.

It was something they couldn't really help; their equipment was mostly secondhand, after all. And they weren't lodging in a place where they could lock their rooms properly, so they needed to carry valuables with them. Because of that, whether they were here in the tavern or out in Damuro, they dressed the same. Frankly, they were a little filthy.

"You people, have you thought about it at all?" Ranta tapped his index finger on the table. "'We're rookies, and Renji was on another level from us to begin with, so there's no helping it,' is that it? Well, let me tell you something: Situations change, got it?"

Moguzo leaned in, looking at Ranta with upturned eyes. "...What do you mean, 'situations'?"

"From what I hear, some new people came in. The group before us was just three people. Incredibly, they still haven't bought their badges. They were a bunch of oddballs, and no one knows what they're off doing now. In our group, there were twelve, right? Well, this time, there's even more, apparently. They're all at the guilds taking the beginners' lessons, and they should be close to finishing soon. Eventually, they'll form parties, and they may even come to Damuro."

"Nothin' wrong with that." Yume puffed out her lips. "If lotsa people come, lotsa people come. With just Yume and everyone there,

Yume worries what'll happen if things go bad. Also, couldn't everyone cooperate to take on larger groups of gobbies?"

That was one way of looking at it...but—Haruhiro couldn't take the arrival of newcomers as positively as Yume.

Setting Merry aside for the moment, Haruhiro and his group had been volunteer soldiers for the shortest amount of time. So it was inevitable that their party was small and weak.

What Ranta was saying was right. Haruhiro, at least, was aware of it.

*However, that's going to change,* he thought. *There will be people who came after us soon. If we keep on taking it easy, they might get ahead of us. Wouldn't that be kind of pathetic...?*

"I think it's best not to rush," Merry said, as if seeing through Haruhiro's feelings.

*Yeah...she's right,* he thought. *Rushing won't do any good. In the end, we can only do what we can do. Those who can skip a step or two, climbing the stairs at a quicker pace, are free to do so, but it doesn't seem like that's something we're capable of. If we tried and failed, we could hope to just suffer some bruises, but the fact of the matter is that we could die.*

*We should take it step by step, slowly but surely.* But—here, Haruhiro had some doubts. *Are we really climbing up step by step? Maybe we're not climbing, but marching in place...?*

"Here's an idea." Haruhiro couldn't even look anyone in the eye, so he dropped his gaze to the table. "...Now, this is just an example, but we can't keep hunting goblins forever, so we could try going to another place... I don't think it would be a terrible idea, right? Though we don't have to suddenly change our hunting grounds entirely. But being in the same place all the time, it becomes...routine, you might say. It turns into routine work, and we may make odd mistakes because of that. I think we need stimulation, you know. It's just an example, though."

"Haruhiroooo." Ranta gave him a full-faced grin. "Buddy, once in a long while, you say good stuff. Just once in a *really* long while, though. Of course, I'm in favor of that plan!"

"Well, Yume's against it, then."

"Okay—I am, too..." Shihoru said.

In seeing how fast Yume and Shihoru joined the opposition, Ranta's lack of virtue was on explosive display.

"Muh..." Moguzo made a difficult expression, and he seemed to be deep in thought.

*What about Merry?* Haruhiro couldn't read anything from her expression or mannerisms, so he didn't know.

"Anyway, it wasn't a plan..." Haruhiro said, scratching the back of his head. "Just an example, like I said. Like, this is one way of looking at it, you know? But we've walked to pretty much every corner of Damuro, so I think there's the issue of what to do next."

"What to do next, huh?" Yume grabbed her braids and wrapped them around her neck. "So long as we're good for today, Yume thinks that's good enough. Is doin' the same thing every day so bad? Lately, we don't get into trouble no more, and we're puttin' away a bit of money. Yume doesn't really have anythin' to complain about."

"Do you have no drive for self-improvement?" Ranta clicked his tongue. "You aren't even human anymore. A pig, that's what you are. A pig."

"Piglets are cute, you know! But, well, piglets grow up to be pigs, and pigs, they aren't as cute as piglets are. So, Yume thinks it's okay if piglets stay as piglets."

"Huh? What are you even saying? What're piglets suddenly entering the conversation for? I don't get it at all," Ranta fumed.

"You don't get it because you're a dummy, Ranta. That's not Yume's fault."

"Don't blame other people! Also, I'm not a dummy! If anyone's a dummy here, it's you!"

"Dummy, dummy, dummy."

"Why, you!"

"C-cut it out, you two..." Moguzo tried to stop them, but it was a pretty reserved attempt, so it didn't have much effect.

Haruhiro brought the wooden mug to his lips for a sip of lemonade. *Am I rushing things? Of course I am. Team Renji is on such a different level, I don't even feel like trying to catch up. Or, rather, I could never feel like catching up. I won't ask to be like them, but if you ask me whether we're okay the way we are now, well... I wonder about that. If new people come along and then they get ahead of us, I don't think I'd be fine with that. It would probably eat at me a little. Or maybe a lot.*

*But I get what Yume is saying, as well.*

*What is our goal? Realistically, it's to keep ourselves alive for now. To carry on with our lives. To live as well as we can.*

*Now that we've bought our badges, we can use the lodging house free of charge. It's rundown, but being able to sleep in a place that keeps us out of the rain is a big deal. If we choose where we eat carefully, we can keep the cost of eating down, too. If we must cut back, there are any number of ways we can do so. But that's stifling. I want to stay in better lodgings. If I could rent a room with a lock on a ten-day or monthly basis, that would be so wonderful. Then I'd have a place I could feel safe about leaving my stuff. I'd even be able to have more personal belongings.*

*If we keep going to Damuro like this and save up, we can probably reach those sorts of goals eventually. There's no need to push ourselves. What would we do if we overextend ourselves and something awful happens?*

*We might die.*

*No.*

*Not might.*

*We actually will die.*

*—Manato.*

*I don't want to let anyone else die. I don't want a repeat of what happened to Manato. We need to be cautious.*

*That said, are we really fine as we are? When I think about it, ever since we bought our badges, we haven't learned new spells and skills or bought better weapons and armor. We've just been aimlessly going to and from Damuro.*

*We successfully avenged Manato, slaying the armored goblin and the hobgoblin. After that, we bought badges and gave one as an offering at Manato's grave.*

*When there was a clear goal, we had drive. There was a sense of tension, a drive to improve ourselves, like Ranta was talking about. We had to become stronger, learn to fight better, otherwise we thought we'd never avenge him. Now, those days are over.*

*Mission complete.*

*Is that what it's like, and now everyone's lost their edge because of it? Can I say for sure that that isn't the case?*

*Maybe preserving the status quo is fine. It's just, if we think preserving the status quo is simple, that it's the easy way, couldn't that trip us up eventually?*

"...Um, don't you think it's about time we head back?" Shihoru said hesitantly and, since there were no objections, that was what they ended up doing.

Merry parted with the group when they left Sherry's Tavern.

When the remaining five were on their way back to their lodgings, Haruhiro suddenly stopped. "—Ah. You guys head back without me. I've got a little something to do..."

"A little something?" Yume blinked repeatedly. "What's a 'little something'?"

"Um...uh, the washroom! I want to hit the washroom. I don't think I can hold it until we get back. That's why..."

Ranta snorted. "What, you need to piss? Just whip it out and do your business wherever, then. We'll wait for you."

Why was it only times like this that Ranta showed off a conscientious side everyone knew he didn't have? It was probably unintentional, but Ranta's annoyingness was too much for him to handle.

"I'm not standing outside to piss," Haruhiro said. "I'll find a shop somewhere and borrow their washroom."

"Hmph. There you go acting all refined," Ranta huffed.

Sending Ranta—who infuriated him—and the other three on ahead, Haruhiro turned back the way they had come.

When he headed back to Sherry's Tavern and looked around, he found Merry sitting at the end of the counter. The truth was, when he'd turned around shortly after they'd parted, he'd thought he'd seen her entering the tavern.

Haruhiro approached Merry and pointed to the seat next to her. "Merry. Do you mind if I sit here?"

Merry looked somewhat surprised, but she nodded. "I...don't mind, but weren't you going home?"

"Weren't you, Merry?" Haruhiro sat next to Merry, giving her a slight smile. "What's that you're drinking there?"

Merry looked down in embarrassment, pulling her porcelain mug in closer to herself. "Mead. I thought I'd go for one more round."

"Mead...that's alcohol made from honey, right? Maybe I'll have some of that, too."

Once Haruhiro paid one of the waitresses and ordered mead, he suddenly found himself unable to speak.

*I did come here looking for Merry. And, yes, Merry's here, but...I have something to talk to her about, something I want to ask for her advice on. I meant to ask Merry for advice with this, but it's something that's hard to talk about with everyone here. Even without everyone here, it's still hard to talk about it.*

The waitress brought him his drink. It wasn't honey-colored. It had a slight red tinge so perhaps there was something added to it. Haruhiro took a sip. It was sweet, with just a little bit of sourness.

"They add raspberry syrup, I hear," Merry explained.

"Ah, so that's it," he said. "That sounds like what I was tasting. It's good."

"What's up?"

"Yeah..."

In the end, he couldn't broach the topic by himself. *I'm hopeless,* Haruhiro thought. *I can't keep being like this.*

"Merry, you've been in a lot of parties before now, right? So, I had something I wanted to ask. Ah..."

Merry had a difficult expression on her face. That was what it looked like.

*I messed up,* Haruhiro realized.

Merry hadn't let go of her past; there was no sign of the positive, always-smiling person who she had once been. But even so, she was doing her best as a member of Haruhiro's party. If she didn't want to remember the past anymore, it wouldn't be strange at all for her to feel that way.

*I shouldn't have brought that up.*

Merry, however, gave a slight nod. "Don't worry about me. It's fine."

"...You sure? If you're forcing yourself, well, that's not good... So, I'd rather you didn't. Uh, wait, I'm the one who brought it up, so it's weird for me to be saying that."

"What is it you want to ask?" Merry's expression was a little stiff. Or maybe it just looked that way. Maybe Haruhiro was overthinking things. But if he stopped here, that would be awkward in and of itself.

"I was wondering, what do you think of our party? Like, what we're capable of. No...what do you think *I'm* capable of?"

"What *about* you, Haru?"

"Well, it's weird for me to say this, but you know, I'm the leader, or something like that?"

"'Something like that'? Aren't you the leader?"

"...Maybe I am the leader. Have I been acting leader-y enough?"

Merry lowered her eyes, thinking for a moment before opening her mouth. "From what I've seen, I think leaders can be broadly divided into two types."

"What are those two types?"

"The dictator type and the chairman type. I just came up with the names, so don't think too much about them."

"Right. The dictator type...they're like, 'I am strong,' and they pull everyone along with them. Something like that?" Haruhiro ventured.

"Yeah. With that type, they tend to be strong personalities, with the ability to force other people to obey them with no room for objection. The party fundamentally does whatever they want. Anyone who goes against them is punished, or expelled, so people who are dissatisfied can't stay in that party for long."

*Renji's that type of leader,* Haruhiro thought. *Though, I'm pretty sure no one would ever go against Renji.*

"The chairman type isn't like that, they're...what? The type that irons out differences?" he asked.

"Yes. Because they're likable or good at speaking, they're the type that's good at bringing everyone around to the same point of view. With this type, they don't necessarily have to be strong. Sometimes, they almost seem like they're there just for show. Like, people may wonder why that person is the leader at first glance. However, even when there's conflict within the party, it often gets neatly resolved thanks to that person."

"I see. The dictator and the chairman. Hmm. I'm..."

*Definitely not the dictator type,* he thought. *Then am I the chairman type? But I'm not especially well-liked, and I'm not a very good talker. You couldn't call me unique, I'm not strong-willed, and I don't have the power to make others submit, either. I'm missing everything I need to be a dictator, so if I'm going to aspire to one, it should be the chairman. I guess that's about the sum of it.*

*What was it like for Manato, I wonder? It was clear he was at the top of the party. Even so, he never tried to force us to follow him. We all just listened to what Manato said, naturally letting him guide us.*

"...Is there something in between the two?" he asked.

"I *told* you I was dividing them broadly. These aren't meant to be narrow categories. While one leader may be the archetypical dictator, another leader may have elements of both the dictator and the chairman, deciding which to use depending on the situation."

"Basically, everyone's different. Is that it?"

"Right. Sorry if that wasn't of much use to you."

"No, that's not true. If we're talking about types, I'd be the chairman, right? If I had to be one of the two."

"That's what I think."

"Hmm..." Haruhiro looked up to the ceiling. "Well, as a chairman, you know, I wish people would assert themselves more. Like, 'I want to do this,' or 'I want to do that.' Or, like, 'I think we should do this.' I mean, in our group, the only one who's clear about that stuff is Ranta. The rest of us—myself included—are passive, you could say. We're the type who easily go with the flow."

"Do you feel lost?" she asked.

"I wouldn't say I don't feel lost, I guess. Ahh. See, I tend to be vague, like just now."

Merry's lips loosened just a little.

*You know,* Haruhiro thought with renewed admiration, *Merry sure is beautiful.*

And here he was, alone together with her.

*When I think about it too much, it makes me feel weird. It's uncomfortable. Is it really okay for me to be here? I start to think it's not appropriate for me to be with her.*

"...Like 'no one invited you,' maybe?" he murmured.

"Did you say something?" Merry asked.

"Huh? Did you hear something? Maybe you just imagined it...?" Haruhiro put on a fake smile. *Whoops, what I was thinking slipped out. I really don't have it together. I need to be more steady. As the leader of the party, I need to shape up.*

*Not that I want to do it.*

*It's not like I'm the leader because I wanted to be. I'm just doing it because I had no choice.*

"About what you said earlier," she said. Merry was probably trying to be considerate. Haruhiro was almost forcing her to be.

"Ah, right," Haruhiro put on a more serious expression. "What? What's this I said?"

"About maybe changing our hunting grounds."

"Oh. Yume and Shihoru opposed it, and the conversation went nowhere after that...all thanks to Ranta. Dammit."

"So long as you aren't rushing things, I think that's one option."

*Well, honestly, I am in a bit of a rush.* Haruhiro wished he could say that honestly, but he kept it inside. He didn't want to show Merry too much of his uncool side. Though, it was probably a little late for that.

"I see. Well, if we were to go somewhere else, where would be good?"

"The Cyrene Mines," Merry answered immediately, almost like she'd had it prepared. She said it expressionlessly.

Haruhiro almost said, *"But isn't that where..."* but he bit back the words. *Wasn't that where your comrades died?* he thought. *You fought a dangerous kobold called Death Spots or something, and lost three people.*

*Yes, weren't they the warrior, Michiki, the thief, Ogu, and the mage, Mutsumi? What happened to them after that? It should have been impossible to retrieve the bodies.*

*If they weren't cremated, with No-Life King's curse, the three of them would have...*

*Should I not talk about that? Or would it be better to broach the issue?* Haruhiro couldn't decide.

Ultimately, after asking Merry various things about the kobolds of the Cyrene Mines, he left the tavern for the night.

On his way back to the lodging house, nothing but regrets came to mind, leaving a bitter taste in his mouth.

*I'm so wishy-washy...*

Regardless, it wasn't something he needed to decide right away. He could take his time and think it over carefully.

That had been his plan, but, in the end, he wasn't able to follow it.

*Grimgar of Fantasy and Ash*

# 3. The Inertial Laws of Habit

"...Oh, man. Oh, man. Oh, man. Oh, maaaaan. What the heck is this...?" Ranta muttered with his back pressed firmly against a wall. He was wearing his heaume, a bucket-shaped helmet.

It wasn't just Ranta; Haruhiro and everyone else were right next to him.

"What does this mean...?" Haruhiro looked at Merry, who was next to him.

Merry shook her head slightly. "I don't know, either."

"That's a lotta gobbies..." Yume whispered.

"Y-yeah..." Moguzo pulled his huge body back and shuddered just a little.

Shihoru closed her eyes, clutching her staff tightly. She looked like she was praying. "...We can't do this. We can't. There's no way we can manage this..."

Shihoru was right. They had to accept that this situation was too much for them.

Normally the Old City of Damuro was sparsely populated with

goblins, but for some reason, today was different. As soon as they entered—no, even before they entered—it was clear something was out of the ordinary.

There were a ton of goblins lurking around.

In groups, no less.

The goblins had formed bands.

It was as if they were patrolling the old city.

"...Patrols," Haruhiro said, grinding his teeth. *Maybe...isn't that what they are?* he thought.

These goblins weren't like the ones they usually faced. They had good equipment. On top of that, they were full of energy; the goblins of the Old City usually lazed around until they noticed the party.

*They're probably goblins from the New City,* Haruhiro thought.

A fair number of New City goblins ended up getting exiled to the Old City, but those goblins tended to be kind of apathetic. The armored goblin with the hobgoblin servant had been like that.

These guys, on the other hand, were full of life. They were working towards some goal. Either that, or they were working under someone's orders.

"Hmph," Ranta laughed, trying to act cool.

*He doesn't look cool at all, though,* Haruhiro thought.

"Looks like we overdid it a little here, huh...?" asked Ranta.

No one contradicted him. Of course, that included Haruhiro.

He didn't have the energy to waste on something so pointless. It was too dangerous for them to enter the Old City like this. Even after taking the trouble to come all this way, they would have to go home without being able to accomplish anything.

*No,* Haruhiro thought. *I would have preferred this to be something we decided for ourselves. If I suggest it now, it'll be like suggesting we do it because we have no choice, or something like that. It's a way of doing it that lacks a sense of tension, but maybe we should think of this is a good opportunity.*

"Hey, how about we try going to the Cyrene Mines?" he asked aloud. "It's not really on the way, but it's in the same direction. It looks like we can just divert around Damuro and continue to the northwest."

Ranta looked thrilled, and Yume, Shihoru, Moguzo and Merry didn't present any opposition to the idea.

So, the group went another four kilometers northwest of Damuro. Granted, it was only four kilometers as the crow flies—but this being their first time, the trip there ultimately took them close to two hours.

*The Cyrene Mountain Mines. It looks like any other mountain,* thought Haruhiro when they arrived.

Apparently, these mines had been developed long ago, back when the human kingdom of Arabakia had held power in the frontier. Later, after they had been driven out by the Alliance of Kings led by No-Life King, a faction of kobolds called the Bosh, or something like that, had occupied the mountains. They had lived in the mines ever since.

Once they reached the foothills, the party could see what looked like an entrance to the mines in the distance. It looked like a rectangular tunnel reinforced with wood.

There was a small stream, so they followed it up the mountain and saw a bear. It was a wild animal, and cautious to an almost cowardly degree, so they figured it probably wouldn't attack them. However, there was no guarantee of that, so they decided to avoid it.

On their way up the slope, they came across what seemed to be a game trail in the forest. As they continued along it, they ran into some furry humanoid creatures with dog-like heads.

They carried rusty swords and wore what looked like the tattered remnants of chain mail. There were two of them.

The two stepped out from the shadow of a tree nonchalantly, and the party hadn't been expecting them either, so for two or three seconds, they stood there just looking at each other awkwardly.

"Kobolds...!" Merry shouted.

Haruhiro unintentionally cried out "Whoa!" and jumped backwards.

"Moguzo, we're doing this...!" Ranta slashed at the kobold on the right.

"Y-yeah!" A little after him, Moguzo closed in on the kobold to the left.

Haruhiro pounded his chest. —*Comb down.*

*No. That's not right. It's calm down. Oh, crap! I'm not calm at all.*

"—Shihoru and Merry, fall back for now! Yume, support Ranta and Moguzo...!"

"Fwah!" came Yume's nonsensical response, but she still moved forward with Haruhiro.

"Hah, hah, hah...!" Ranta was furiously exchanging blows with a kobold.

Moguzo was grunting loudly and busily swinging his bastard sword around, but he didn't even touch them.

"Yume, help Moguzo...!" Haruhiro shouted.

"Gotcha!"

Haruhiro took aim at the back of the kobold fighting Ranta. First, he'd take care of one of them quickly, then they'd all gang up on the remaining one. That was the plan.

However...

"H-huh...?"

He couldn't seem to get behind it. He couldn't predict its movements; they were too fast for his eyes to follow.

*What's this? Are kobolds strong? Are they ridiculously fast?* he thought.

"Dammit! Haruhiro, what are you doing...?!" Ranta shouted.

While Ranta was matching blades with the kobold, he didn't seem to be on the attack. If anything, he was being pushed back. Mostly, he was blocking the kobold's attacks with his sword, unable to get off a decent counterattack.

*What about Moguzo and Yume?* Haruhiro thought.

*No, I don't have time to look. First, I need to do something about the kobold in front of me.*

"Don't move around so much, Ranta!" he yelled.

"Oh, shove it! I've got my reasons...!"

"I can't work with you moving so much!"

"Like I care! Whoa...!"

The kobold stepped in close, locking blades with Ranta.

*Good. That'll keep them from moving. Now's my chance.*

"Backstab...!" Haruhiro tried to stab his dagger into its back, but it dodged it.

*That way of dodging it is rather...* The kobold leapt to the side, slapping aside Haruhiro's dagger with a whish of its tail. *...I dunno... tricky?*

"Man, you're useless, Haruhiro!" Ranta chased after the kobold. The kobold met his attack, hopping left and right with irritating dancelike steps.

*That movement style. That's what's giving us so much trouble.*

*Also, when I'm behind it, its tail really catches my eye. It's always moving; I can't help but pay attention to it.*

"...This is tough!" Haruhiro shouted.

It probably wasn't an issue of their opponent being strong or weak. Haruhiro and the others didn't know these enemies. How would their opponents attack? How would they defend? How would they react to different situations? How would they respond to different approaches the party took? There was just too much they didn't know.

"If this were a goblin...!" Haruhiro grunted.

When he took aim at the kobold's back again, like he always did... *That's it,* Haruhiro realized.

In his head, there was always a goblin. He was looking at the kobold's back like it *was* a goblin's. A goblin's physique. A goblin's habits. A goblin's thought processes. Those things were ingrained in him now, and he couldn't wipe them away.

*Have we gotten too used to fighting goblins...?* he wondered.

"Smash...!" Merry suddenly leapt out and smashed her priest's staff into the shoulder of the kobold Moguzo and Yume were fighting.

The kobold yelped and ran away at an incredible speed, barking far off in the distance.

"These are lesser kobolds. They shouldn't be tough opponents by any means!" Merry said, thrusting the pommel of her priest's staff into the ground, causing the rings on it to jingle. "If you keep a level head while fighting, I guarantee you can win this!"

*Yeah!* Haruhiro thought. *Merry, you're so cool.*

"...Wait, I don't have time to stand here and be impressed!" he added out loud.

Haruhiro exchanged a glance with Ranta. He didn't like that they understood one another without words but, technically, they were comrades, so it wasn't hard for them to understand what the other person was thinking at times like this.

*Look closely,* Haruhiro said to himself.

*Observe.*

*It's not a goblin we're fighting. It's a kobold. An unfamiliar enemy. However, it's just unfamiliar. If you think about it, it's not like it's really pushing us hard. That means, like Merry said, it's not a tough opponent.*

"Ohm, rel, ect, vel, darsh...!" Shihoru cast her Shadow Beat spell with its distinctive *vwong.*

The shadow elemental—which looked like a ball of black seaweed—struck the kobold that had come back and was loping towards Yume and Moguzo. The kobold fell to its knees, its entire body convulsing.

"Moguzo, now!" Yume shouted.

Moguzo charged at the kobold with a shout. They had that one covered, which meant Haruhiro could focus on the other one.

"There! Take that! And that!" Ranta shouted. He was irritatingly loud, but unlike before, he wasn't just swinging his longsword around randomly. He was watching the kobold's moves closely. When the kobold went right, he went right. When it went left, he went left. He wasn't able to get ahead of it, but the kobold wasn't running circles around him. He wasn't just defending anymore; he could attack occasionally, too.

*Thanks to that, the kobold doesn't have attention to spare elsewhere,* Haruhiro thought.

Now, I can get there. Behind it.

*Don't let its tail distract me. In the end, it's just a tail.*

*Goblins are like humans, but kobolds move in a wilder, beast-like way. Kobolds seem like they have strong legs. They've got spring, which gives them jumping strength. That's why they feel faster than goblins.*

*But how long it takes them to do things—their reaction time, their reflexes and whatnot—probably isn't much different. When it comes to how flexible their bodies are, goblins probably have them beat. If I look closely, when the kobolds lean forward, their upper body doesn't move much. They swing their swords differently from how goblins do, too. Goblins use their entire body to swing, but kobolds only use their arms. They swing their arms like whips. Maybe they have stiff shoulders. They're probably about 150 cm tall. That's a little bigger than a goblin, but the goblin probably swings harder.*

*Though, compared to goblins—who use their whole body for big moves—kobolds' attacks are more compact. That makes them faster. If I fight them like I would a goblin, I'll always end up acting later than they do.*

While there were a lot of differences, the kobold wasn't always superior. Haruhiro and the party could take on up to five goblins simultaneously. Right now, they were facing two kobolds.

*We can win. Actually, there's no way we can't win!*

That wasn't overconfidence speaking. It was the answer his experience and observations had led him to.

*It's amazing,* thought Haruhiro. Once he calmed down and started to believe he could do this, his field of vision widened. Until moments ago, he had only been able to see the kobold in front of him and Ranta, but now he could keep track of the movements of the rest of his comrades.

"Thanks...!" Moguzo cut down one of the kobolds, swinging his sword down diagonally with all his might in a Rage Blow.

*When the other kobold sees that, it'll probably shake it up,* Haruhiro thought.

*It did.*

*Right now, it's not watching its back at all.*

Haruhiro held his breath and threw his full weight against the kobold's back. Of course, he did more than just tackle it. Backstab. He stabbed it with his dagger. Deeply, through a tear in its chainmail.

The kobold let out a yelp.

Haruhiro immediately leapt away from it.

"Heck, yeah...!" Ranta stepped in, thrusting out his longsword. "Anger!"

*It went through.* Ranta's longsword struck the kobold in the gullet. The kobold collapsed, unable to utter a sound.

Haruhiro breathed out. "...We won."

"It's all thanks to me!" Ranta boasted, hoisting his sword high.

"Nuh-uh, no it isn't," Yume looked exasperated. "No matter how you look at it, it was thanks to Merry. What she said back there, that was super cool. 'If you keep a level head while fighting, I guarantee you can win this,' she said. It gave Yume the little zap she needed to get her going."

"S-stop it..." Merry looked down. Her face was a little red. "...I'm sorry for butting in. It wasn't my place to say that."

"Th-that's not...!" Shihoru spoke in a loud voice, which was uncommon for her. "That's not...true, I think. I don't think you have anything to apologize for..."

"Y-yeah," Moguzo nodded slowly. "It helped me find my courage."

"You're all a bunch of small-fry!" said Ranta.

*How could Ranta be so full of himself?* Haruhiro wondered. Was it because he was an idiot?

"You can't find your courage without someone giving you a pep talk? You're all crap, you know that? Crap!"

Haruhiro deliberately ignored Ranta, crouching down in front of one of the kobolds' dead bodies. "Let's see, their weapons and armor don't look like they're worth anything, but...looks like it's wearing something. A nose ring, I guess you'd call it. It's made out of an animal's fang or something."

Like a priest mourning the dead, Merry made the sign of the hexagram and then crouched down next to Haruhiro. "Those are talismans. Every kobold always has one."

"Hmm. But it doesn't look all that valuable," Haruhiro said.

"The kobolds living in the first level of the mines are the outcasts of their society. They're dressed poorly, and they have meager physiques. That's why volunteer soldiers call them lesser kobolds," she said.

"So, does that mean non-lesser kobolds have better talismans, then?"

"Yes. Made from pretty stones, or metal. Even lesser kobolds occasionally use humans' copper and silver coins to make talismans."

"I see. Then, if we fight a lesser one and it has a silver coin or something, we can consider ourselves lucky," he mused.

Merry was being rather talkative. That alone was enough to make Haruhiro really happy.

"Well, for now let's snag it anyway," Ranta said. He tore the nose ring off the kobold's corpse. "—Huh? What?" he said, glaring at a disapproving Haruhiro.

"Nothing..." Haruhiro replied.

*I know we have to retrieve the loot,* he thought, *but aren't there better ways he could do it? I know it's weird to say that after killing them, and all. But—*

*That's right, isn't it? From the kobolds' perspective, we're like invaders.*

What Haruhiro and the others were doing was slaughter, and even if he felt some pangs of conscience over it, that fact didn't change. Whether he gently cut the nose ring from the dead body or violently tore it off, it was the same in the end.

When he looked at Ranta, it was like looking at an image of himself stripped of all pretense, and that was hard to bear.

Ranta acted without hesitation, but Haruhiro tried to keep up appearances. Perhaps his way of thinking was nothing more than hypocrisy.

Even so, when Haruhiro removed an earring that had been made from polished horn or something similar from the other kobold, he tried to do as little damage to the corpse as possible. He wouldn't consider changing his methods. Even if they were his enemies—his *prey*—there was a bare minimum of respect that had to be shown.

Haruhiro stood up.

"Let's go," he said. "To the Cyrene Mines."

## 4. The Ways of Darkness

*Since they call them mines,* Haruhiro had thought, *there're probably tunnels that have been dug into the mountain. In those tunnels, it'll be pitch black, of course.* That was what he'd thought, but his expectations were betrayed.

*There are flowers,* he thought in surprise. Flowers are blooming here and there in the tunnel.

These weren't just any flowers; they gave off an emerald glow. According to Merry, they were apparently called lightflowers, which was exactly what they were.

On closer examination, they weren't flowers so much as plants that were made out of moss, but, regardless, thanks to them, the tunnels weren't dark. They still couldn't be called bright, but the party could see, for the most part.

"But, you know, these things—" Ranta said, picking a lightflower and sticking it in his mouth.

*What is he thinking?* Haruhiro thought.

Ranta immediately spat it back out with a disgusted noise. "Yuck!

That's nasty. It's bitter. So bitter I could puke! You can't eat this stuff. Ugh! Yuck! Bleh, bleh, bleh."

Haruhiro sighed. "...What are you doing?"

"Huh?" Ranta wiped his mouth and said, "Trying to eat it, obviously."

"Why would you eat it...?"

"Don't you get it? It felt like we had a bad mood going on here, so I did it to try to help you all chill out."

"That's never going to help anyone chill out, and the mood is totally normal. If it's bad, then that's probably your fault," Haruhiro said.

"Huh? Don't give me that bullshit. Why would it be my fault? Don't try to blame everything on other people."

"Don't do it, Haru-kun," Yume pulled on Haruhiro's sleeve. "Ranta doesn't hear a word people say to him. Tryin' to have a conversation with him is just wastin' your time."

Haruhiro nodded. "Yeah. You're right."

"—Wait! Hold on! Hey!" Ranta protested.

"We should keep quiet," Merry gave Ranta a quiet glare. "We're already in enemy territory, you realize."

Ranta arched his eyebrows and screwed up his face. It was a terrible expression. "Yeah, yeah, yeah, yeah. I just gotta be quiet, right? *Real* quiet. The rest of you shut up, too. Don't say a word. You got that? Well?"

"...He's like a child," Shihoru whispered.

That made a vein bulge on Ranta's temple. "What'd you say...?"

"Enough already!" Haruhiro yelled despite himself. "We're not here to play around. If this goes badly, someone could *die*, okay?"

Ranta looked to the side awkwardly. "...I know that. It's not hard to figure out. You don't have to tell me."

"Do you really get it...?" Haruhiro snapped.

*He really makes me mad.* Haruhiro thought. *I'm so angry I don't know what to do. Is this okay? Can we really keep Ranta in the party like this?*

*If I consider what's best for the party, wouldn't it be better to chase him out? It's not that I can't count on him to contribute in battle, and it's not like he isn't useful, but...he causes trouble over every little thing. He irritates all of us. It's becoming stressful. Is he more of a negative than a positive, maybe? Is he a hindrance?*

*That's not something to think about right now, I guess. Though...if I say that...when am I going to make the decision?*

They proceeded down the tunnel, finding a group of three lesser kobolds. Their opponents seemed frightened, but didn't run away, so they fought them. When Moguzo downed one, and Ranta another, the third one suddenly fled.

It had a unique way of running. Kobolds usually walked upright on two feet, but this one also used the hand it didn't have a weapon in for running. This made it pretty fast. They had a hard time catching up to it and they were worried as they did. If other kobolds attacked while they were pursuing it, they'd be in trouble. Fortunately, they managed to avoid that happening, but they'd need to keep how quickly the kobolds could run away in mind.

*There's a lot we're uncertain about,* Haruhiro thought, *but we'll just have to get used to kobolds the way we got used to goblins. It's a matter of building up experience points.*

"The Cyrene Mines have more than ten levels, and—" The way

Merry's voice echoed through the tunnel, it sounded like it was seeping into his heart. "The ore veins on the first level have long since been exhausted. Basically, there's nothing but lightflowers, so the lesser kobolds live here. There was a vertical shaft in the back at one point, but it was buried by a cave-in, and now you have to go down through wells to reach the second level."

"Wells...?" Shihoru asked.

"Yes," Merry responded, with a nod. "Wells. Though, that's just what volunteer soldiers call them. Basically, they're vertical holes. From the third level down, there are vertical shafts with elevators installed in them, but we primarily use wells to go up and down."

Moguzo gave a nasal, "Hmm," and then asked, "Is it because security is tight...?"

"Yes. With kobolds, there are three types: lesser kobolds, normal kobolds, and elder kobolds, which are larger. Only the elder kobolds can use the elevators freely. Normal kobolds can only use the elevators when they are permitted or ordered by an elder kobold to do so."

"It's soundin' like these elders act real bossy," Yume said. Knowing Yume, she was probably sympathizing with the other kobolds.

Merry smiled faintly. "The leaders are the ruling class and the normal kobolds are the workers, while the lesser kobolds aren't even seen as self-sufficient. The second level is the living space for the lowest of the laborers—the low workers—so think of that as where things will get started for real."

"Up ahead then, huh?" Haruhiro licked his lips to moisten them.

He and the others had stopped in front of an open vertical hole.

*This is it: a well,* he thought.

At a guess, he'd have placed the hole at about 3 meters in diameter.

It was a bit irregular, but the hole was mostly round, and there were four rope ladders attached to it.

*Do we go? Or not?*

While Haruhiro was swallowing his spit and agonizing over it, Ranta started to climb down the ladder.

"Wait, aren't you rushing in a bit...?" Haruhiro asked.

"Huh?" Ranta narrowed his eyes. "Come on, quit dragging your feet! After coming this far, is not going even an option? It isn't, is it? Like it ever could be. Let's get going, you bunch of buffoons. I'll leave you behind, you got that?"

"Actually, I almost *want* to leave you behind here..." Haruhiro murmured.

"Try it, and I'll kill you. Seriously, I'll do it!"

*Well, nothing else for it, then.* Haruhiro descended one of the rope ladders.

The second level was rather different from the first. It had originally been a mine level, of course, but there were countless holes dug into the sides of the walls, and it looked like there were residences—or rather, dens—inside them.

Well, it more than just looked like it. When Haruhiro peeked into, there were kobolds snoring away which surprised him a little.

"...W-won't we be in trouble if they wake up?" he muttered. "There's a good number of kobolds just in this hole..."

Just then, he heard a dog-like barking in the distance. That's what it sounded like but he quickly realized it was the kobolds were quarreling among themselves.

*Is there a fight going on?* he wondered.

The barking quickly faded, but then he heard more from another direction.

"It's pretty noisy, huh?" Yume didn't seem that frightened.

"...May..." Shihoru clung to Yume, trembling. "...Maybe we should turn back...?"

"It's fine," Merry said in a calm voice. "They're always noisy like this, so once the low workers are sleeping, they won't wake up unless something really major happens. Even if we make a little bit of a scene, it's rare for many of them to gather."

"Oh..." Moguzo said, as he took a breath.

"That's only true as deep as this level, though," Merry said with a little laugh. "Because, from the third level down, there are elders. We have to be careful with them. Also, there's the one that has the spots of death—Death Spots."

The moment they heard that name, it wasn't just Haruhiro who got spooked. Even Ranta's expression went a little stiff.

With black and white spotted fur, it had a body bigger than an elder, apparently. This extremely vicious super-kobold went around the mines with a small group of underlings.

The "Spots" in its name came from its spots, while the "Death" came from its having killed scores of volunteer soldiers. Among its victims were Merry's former comrades.

She must have felt she needed to kill Death Spots to avenge her friends. If someone had managed to slay it, people would have been guaranteed to talk about it. Since that hadn't happened, that meant it was still alive.

"It will even appear on the first level sometimes, is what they say." Strangely, Merry's tone didn't change.

*Isn't she just forcing herself to keep up a calm façade?* Haruhiro couldn't help but think.

"We don't have any trustworthy reports of it being sighted there, so I don't think we need to think about that for now," Merry said. "However, from the second level down, it's a different matter. You need to keep Death Spots in mind. If it comes at us, we need to run right away, or—"

"This," Ranta grinned and made a gesture like his throat was being clawed out. "That's what'll happen to us, right?"

"Oh, jeez!" Yume slapped Ranta on the shoulder.

"Ow. Wh-what?"

"How can you be so darn insensitive?!" Yume demanded.

"Huh? How am I insensitive? I don't think you'll find a person out there as sensitive as I am!"

"Drink before you speak!"

"...Yume, it's 'think before you speak', okay?" Haruhiro corrected her. But he regretted it a little; it felt like he'd interrupted her when she was trying to say something.

Clearing his throat loudly, he looked over at Merry. *Merry's acting like she's fine. I expected that, but I don't know whether she really is or not. She seems like the type to bottle her feelings up inside her, so I'm worried.*

"Anyway, Ranta, shut up for a bit," Haruhiro said. "If you have to talk, at least say something better."

"Fine, then let me suggest something better." Ranta used his chin to gesture towards the hole where the low worker kobolds were sleeping. "Those guys don't wake easily, right? In that case, why don't we just kill the lot of them in their sleep and score some easy loot? Let's snuff 'em, quick and easy."

Haruhiro was speechless for a moment. "...Are you a demon?"

"Tch, tch, tch." Ranta waggled his index finger back and forth while clicking his tongue. "I'm no demon. I'm a knight of darkness, a dread knight. Understand? I serve the dark god Skullhell! 'All are equal before death' is part of our philosophy. The vices that we value are the antithesis of the meaningless platitudes *you* people call morals and common sense. Their antithesis. It's important, so I'll say it a third time: their antithesis.

"I mean, anyway, we're all going to die someday. So doesn't it feel stupid letting yourself be tied down by all that stuff? If there's one thing we should be beholden to, it's our desires. Our instincts, impulses, that sort of stuff. At the end of it all, the equality of death awaits. Understand?"

"I don't understand at all, and I don't want to."

"Haruhiroooo...you should get a little more training, you know? For that head of yours. You can't serve as leader with that low level of comprehension, can you? Let me just say: I'm warning you out of the goodness of my own heart here, you know?"

*...Wow. What should I do?* Haruhiro thought. *What's the right thing to do? I really want to slug him.*

Had Ranta ended up like this because his mind was poisoned by the dread knights? At the very least, there had to be more to it than that. After all, Ranta had originally meant to be a warrior. Warriors were indispensable to the party, so he'd volunteered for the position. Despite that, because he thought they were cooler—or something like that—and without telling Haruhiro and the others, he'd gone and become a dread knight. Ranta had always been a selfish and unreasonable guy. It was his personality. His nature.

*Ranta's never going to get better,* Haruhiro thought. *He won't change. He'll always be like this. Can I keep working with a guy like this? To be totally honest, I'm not confident I can. But is that something I should have to be confident about? For a guy like Ranta?*

*It's not something to decide on right here and now, though, I know. If I just said, "We don't need you anymore, see ya," and broke up with him right here, somehow, I feel like that'd put me on his level.*

"Your suggestion's rejected. I don't think we even need to take a vote," Haruhiro said.

Everyone nodded. Everyone but Ranta.

"Pft," he snorted. "Yeah, I thought it might be like that."

"Then don't say it in the first place..."

"I'm going out of my way to suggest the things that won't even occur to you. Can't you understand it? My fatherly love."

"What kind of father are you?" Haruhiro cried.

*I can't get along with this guy,* he thought. *Or, rather, I really shouldn't.*

Haruhiro and the party progressed through the second level. There were apparently five wells down to the third level from the second. For now, they headed towards one of them, and—

*Are these guys coming back from work?* Haruhiro thought.

—they bumped right into a group of low worker kobolds carrying pickaxes and shovels. Four, in total.

"Four...that's a lot!" Haruhiro reflexively stabbed at one of the low workers. When he did, it swung its shovel to block Haruhiro's dagger. It quickly went on the attack.

Shovel. Shovel. Shovel. A flurry of shovel blows.

Haruhiro went swat, swat, swat; he responded with the thief fighting skill that targeted an enemy's weapon and swatted the blow away.

*It damages my dagger, so I don't want to use it too often,* he thought. *But I guess I can't afford to say that now. What about the others? Moguzo, Ranta and Yume look like they're taking on one each.*

There was a stalemate that lasted a few seconds.

"Ohm, rel, ect, vel, darsh...!"

*Vwong.* Shihoru hit the low worker Moguzo was fighting with Shadow Beat. The low worker's body convulsed, rendering it defenseless for a moment.

Moguzo did not miss the opportunity. "Thanks...!"

There it was. Rage Blow, a.k.a. the Thanks Slash.

Haruhiro had no sense for how he'd grown as a fighter, but he felt that Moguzo's slashes had definitely gotten sharper and more precise. With a splat, the low worker crumpled.

Moguzo immediately went to help Yume.

*Good. We can do this—*

Something bumped Haruhiro in the back.

"Whuh?! Haruhiro, dammit!" Ranta shouted.

"Ranta?! Watch where you're going—"

"I could say the same to you!"

"I'm sorry!"

"As long as you get it!"

*He complains about every little thing, and it pisses me off. Even when I was apologizing. What's his problem?*

"Thanks!" Moguzo cut another one down with a Thanks Slash.

That freed up Yume and Moguzo so Ranta shouted, "I'm fine! I've got this! Go help stupid Haruhiro!"

"Who're you calling stupid?!" Haruhiro yelled.

*Give me a break already! I've had it up to here with this. I can't
believe you. You're the worst! Just the worst!*

Haruhiro could feel the blood rising to his head, but he had to
control himself. Moguzo and Yume were coming. The low worker
turned to face them.

*It's back. I can get behind it. Now.*

"Backstab...!"

*That didn't feel like a good hit. Bone. My blade struck bone.*

Haruhiro clicked his tongue and jumped away. Even so, the low
worker seemed concerned about the wound in its back, and it ended
up looking like it might turn around, or might not.

Then Moguzo attacked. "Thanks...!"

*That's his third one.*

The Thanks Slash struck again, to explosive results. The low
worker's right shoulder looked like it'd burst open.

"Moguzo, you're amazing!" Yume shouted out in joy.

*He really was,* Haruhiro thought.

He was strong, but not very clever. Some people might have
thought him slow and stupid, but Moguzo was earnest and single-
minded. Even as he accepted the enemy's blows on his bastard
sword and armor, he looked for an opening. Otherwise, he locked
blades with them and used his skill Wind or brute force to make his
opponent falter, breaking their stance. Then, he finished them with
the Thanks Slash.

He didn't have a lot of variation, but by repeating those same
moves without ever tiring, he'd become polished at it. Moguzo was
the party member who had grown the most.

"Exhaust...!" Ranta retreated backwards so fast he looked like he might take off into the air.

As if being sucked in, the low worker moved up.

Ranta thrust out his longsword. "Anger...!"

The low worker yelped, twisting aside and avoiding the blade, so Ranta backed away further.

"Exhaust...!"

As if being sucked in, the low worker...did not move forward.

*Yeah, of course it wouldn't,* Haruhiro thought. *It's not that stupid.*

"Dammit! Fine, then!" Ranta leapt in, swinging his longsword down diagonally. "Hatred...!"

There was a bark and a clang as the low worker deflected Ranta's longsword with its pickaxe.

Ranta took two or three steps backwards and then exhaled. "You're not half bad. For a mutt, that is. I don't mind recognizing you. You're my rival...!"

The low worker bared its fangs. "Grrrrr...!"

"Oh..." Shihoru whispered disinterestedly, "Your rival, huh..."

"It's a matter of feeling!" Ranta shouted angrily.

*What kind of feeling?* Haruhiro couldn't help but wonder, but he kept his mouth shut. He felt it'd be stupid to say any more.

"But! This next one will finish you!" Ranta jumped at the low worker. "Anger...!"

With a yelp, the low worker dodged the blow and struck back at Ranta.

Ranta ran away. It was Exhaust.

Avoid. Miss.

Hatred. Exhaust.

Anger. Exhaust.

Anger then Exhaust.

Hatred followed by Exhaust.

Anger. Exhaust.

Hatred. Exhaust.

Hatred. Exhaust.

Anger. Exhaust.

Exhaust.

Exhaust. Exhaust.

Exhaust, Exhaust, Exhaust.

"...Hahh, hahh, hahh, hahh." Ranta was wheezing. Of course he was. After chaining that many skills that required a lot of moving around, there was no way he wouldn't be tired.

"Shouldn't someone help...?" Merry looked to Haruhiro and asked.

Ranta's bloodshot eyes went wide. "I don't need your help! This guy is my rival! My prey! I'll take him down! Me! When I say I'll do something, I do it! You all go have a nice time sipping tea or something!"

*Why does he have to get so serious about it?* Haruhiro realized he could probably spend five centuries pondering the question and still not understand. "We don't even have any tea..." he muttered.

"It was a metaphor, dammit! Hatred...!"

The low worker yelped in pain.

*He finally scratched it.*

The low worker was pulling back.

Ranta swung his longsword at it several times in rapid succession. "Take that, and that, and that, and that...!"

The low worker cried out with each blow.

Ranta wasn't so much cutting it up as pummeling it. The low worker must have been totally exhausted. It couldn't dodge. With one final blow to the head, it yelped and collapsed.

"Die...!" Ranta stabbed his longsword into the fallen low worker's chest, giving it a hearty twist before pulling it out. "Whew..."

When he wiped his brow with an expression that seemed to say *All in a day's work,* it was honestly pretty off-putting. In many ways, Haruhiro couldn't help but be repulsed.

He shook his head lightly. *I dunno...*

*What am I going to do, seriously? I know I can't do anything now.*

"...Well, should we collect the loot and move on?" Haruhiro asked.

"That's all you have to say?!" Ranta whined. "Don't you have a compliment?! Like, 'Good work' or 'That was special, Ranta' or 'That was great, Ranta' or 'That was fantastic, Ranta-sama'?!"

"Yeah, no."

"Trip!"

Ignoring Ranta as he did an exaggerated faceplant, Haruhiro collected the talismans from the fallen low workers. Unlike lesser kobolds, the low workers had what looked like gemstones embedded in their earrings and nose rings. *These look like they'll fetch a high price,* he thought.

Ranta had made things harder for himself for no good reason, but having taken down four low workers was an achievement. Haruhiro continued advancing towards the well.

To reach the well down to the third level, with everything involved, it had taken about thirty minutes.

After defeating three low workers as they came up out of the well, they started to discuss what they should do next.

"What do we do? We go down, of course!" Ranta asked.

In a flash, the other five came to an agreement.

"Let's head back for today," Haruhiro said. "We have to take the road back, and I'm starting to get the false impression that we're used to this place when we *really* aren't. We should go rest, clear our heads, and come back tomorrow."

Of course, Ranta fiercely opposed the idea, but Haruhiro didn't care.

*Deciding what to do with you is the biggest problem,* he thought bitterly.

Grimgar
of
Fantasy and Ash

## 5. Capacity

They returned to Alterna before sundown, selling the loot from five lesser kobolds and seven low workers to a buyer near the market. But they only made a little over seven silver.

"Wow..." Yume looked at the seven silver coins and handful of brass ones with a sad look on her face. "This's kinda iffy, y'know..."

"It's more than just iffy..." Ranta's cheek twitched a little. "This is pitiful! Seriously...seriously..."

Moguzo laughed uncomfortably. "I...I expected a little more, y'know...?"

"Yeah." Shihoru hung her head. "...I thought it would be more profitable than hunting goblins..."

"W-well—" Haruhiro tried to address his comrades, but he just couldn't find the right words.

"Today was just normal kobolds," Merry quickly chimed in with a calm, clear voice. "If we take on elders, I think that will pay more."

Haruhiro quickly nodded, "Y-yeah, she's right. Yep. Well, you know...we didn't struggle that much, either, you know? We were a bit awkward at first, but we didn't take any real wounds, so we had room to push ourselves more. We only put in a little effort, so that's why we only earned a little, don't you think?"

"Let's hope you're right," Ranta snorted derisively. "If it's like this again tomorrow, Haruhiro, you'd better take responsibility for it."

"What's that supposed to mean? 'You'd better take responsibility'?"

"I'm telling you to give me your share, to show some sincerity," Ranta said.

Haruhiro was astonished. "Why should I do that...?"

"Huh? Come on, you were the one who suggested we go to the Cyrene Mines."

"You were okay with it, remember?" Haruhiro reminded him.

"I only approved of the idea. I wasn't the one who suggested it! For the past hundred million years, everyone's known that the guy who suggests doing a thing is the one who's the most responsible for whatever happens."

"Fine, just say whatever you want..."

"Huh? I'm *already* saying whatever I want."

*Yeah, you sure are.* Haruhiro couldn't conjure a retort, and it depressed him. *I know it's nothing to be depressed about, but I can't help it. Am I tired? If I am, it's Ranta's fault.*

Even here—eating dinner at a cheap-but-still-pretty-good stall— every time he spoke to Ranta, it wore him down a little more.

*When I don't want to talk to him, he goes and bugs me about every little thing. That's just the kinda guy Ranta is. Fine, then. If that's how it's gonna be, I'll just ignore him entirely.*

"Hey, Haruhiro," Ranta said.

"..."

"Yo, Haruhiro!"

"..."

"Ahoy, Haruhiro!"

"..."

"Ahoy-hoy!"

"..."

"Why, you!" Ranta started doing a bizarre dance while holding a half-eaten meat skewer. "Ho-ho-hoy, hoy-hoy, ho-ho-hoy, ho-ho-hoy! Ho-ho-hoy, hoy-hoy, ho-ho-hoy, ho-ho-hoy! Ho-ho-hoy, hoy-hoy, ho-ho-hoy, ho-ho-hoy!"

*Well, this is annoying,* Haruhiro thought.

Ranta kicked up his legs in turn, shaking his hips around, but somehow, his upper body barely moved. It looked weird—really weird—to the point that it was actually funny.

Haruhiro turned and looked away. *I'll bet everyone's doing their best not to look at Ranta. But...I can hear someone suppressing a chuckle. Not just one person. A few of them are about ready to start laughing.*

"Pft!" Yume burst out laughing.

"Whoa-ho!" Ranta was thrilled. "Ho-ho-hoy!"

"Pft!" Shihoru couldn't hold it in any longer.

Ranta jumped around. "Ho-ho-ho-hoy, hoy-hoy! Ho-ho-ho-ho-ho-hoy!"

"Gwahah!" Moguzo caved in.

Only Haruhiro and Merry remained. Haruhiro looked at Merry, who was looking downwards, her shoulders shaking. Ranta came up next to her, pressing the attack with his entirely too intense Ho-ho-hoy Dance.

*Merry. It's no good. You're at your limit,* Haruhiro thought.

Merry finally buried her head in her arms at the counter. Come hell or high water, she wasn't going to let him make her laugh.

"Ho-ho-hoy, hoy-hoy! Ho-ho-ho-hoy! Ho-ho-hoy, hoy-hoy! Ho-ho-ho-hoy! Ho-ho-hoy, hoy-hoy! Ho-ho-ho-hoy!"

"...!"

*Hang in there, Merry. You can get through this somehow.*

—Wait, why do we have to fight a battle like this?

Suddenly, the impulse to laugh faded. Haruhiro slipped behind Ranta, kicking him in the back of the knee with the tip of his foot.

"Uwah?!" Having suddenly been kicked in the back of the knee, Ranta turned around and got up in Haruhiro's face. "The hell're you doing?! Haruhiro! I almost had her...!"

"Say it, don't spray it! Man, you're gross."

Ranta deliberately sprayed Haruhiro with spit. "Peh! Peh! Peh! Peh!"

"Eugh! Stop!"

"Who do you think's gonna stop me, moron? Peh, peh, peh, peh, peh, peh!"

Haruhiro wasn't the only victim of Ranta's spittle attack: the rest of their comrades and everyone's food were hit, as well.

*What a disaster.*

What's more, even though everyone else was upset and angry, Ranta seemed to be delighted with himself, which made it all the worse.

Thanks to that, their trip back to the lodging house was the

CAPACITY

worst ever.

That, even in this situation, Ranta could still feel that way showed there was something very wrong with him.

"—Okay!" Ranta declared. "Since the girls are taking the first bath, that means today's gonna be the day I go take a look-see!"

Haruhiro rolled over in his bunk, turning his back on the infuriating Ranta. *I don't even want to respond.*

"Huh? What, Haruhiro? You're not coming? I'll bet you're worrying about silly things like what'll happen if we get caught again. You moron. Moguzo, you're coming, right?"

"...Huh? N-no, I'm not..."

"Why not? Come on. If you don't come, I'm gonna be short a stool to stand on."

"I'm not a stool..."

"But you can act like one! You, sir, can become an *excellent* stool!" Ranta declared.

"I don't want to..."

"At this point, I don't care what you think! Trust me, and go along with it for my convenience! I won't let it end badly for you! Okay?!"

"I-I'm not going."

Faced with an uncharacteristically strong rejection from Moguzo, Ranta seemed dispirited.

"...Fine, then! I see how it is. I'll go by myself and make a brilliant success of this mission. If you regret not coming later, it'll be too late. I'm not gonna care. You fine that?"

"I-I'm fine."

"You're *reeeeeally* fine with it?!"

"I-I said, I'm fine."

"Well, I'm not! Moguzo! If you won't be my footstool, this plan's failed before it's even begun! Come on! Get going! No matter what you say, I'm bringing you with me! ...Damn, you're heavy! If I'm pulling you this hard and you don't even budge, just how heavy are you? Are you a fatso?"

"...Yes, I'm fat, but..."

"Moguzo's not fat," Haruhiro interjected despite himself. "His belly doesn't stick out. He's just big."

"Oh-ho." Ranta slapped Haruhiro's bed. "Finally in the mood for it, huh, Haruhiro? You're hopeless, you know that? Well, let's get going then. Come on, get up already!"

How could Ranta have possibly interpreted what he said to mean *that*? Haruhiro had no clue. *Can someone, please, just get rid of Ranta for me, already?*

*I'm hardly even joking.*

After that, he took a bath once the girls were done. When he returned to the dark room and lay in his bed, Haruhiro kept thinking to himself. *The question is, should I cut him loose, or shouldn't I? In terms of my personal feelings, there are times I wish I didn't have to see Ranta's face anymore. If he'd just go away, I'd probably think it was good riddance.*

Haruhiro was sure he wasn't the only one who felt that way.

*I don't know about Moguzo and Merry, but Yume and Shihoru have a lot of bitter words for Ranta. I'm pretty sure neither of them are the type to say when they dislike or hate things. Despite that, they make a pretty blatant show of hating Ranta. That means Ranta's got to be pretty bad.*

*Still, I can't decide just based on my feelings. After all, I'm the group's leader...right? I need to consider the practical side of things, too.*

*Basically, how is Ranta as an asset in battle? How would it affect the way we fight if we lost him?*

Haruhiro gave it some thought.

*Right now, Ranta's functioning as a second tank after Moguzo. He wears a chain shirt under his leather armor, and he has that bucket helmet, so...well...he's a reasonable choice for the role.*

Although, he reflected, it didn't seem like dread knights usually faced the enemy in straight-up exchanges. They did their best to avoid locking blades and kept their distance. Then they would attack from outside the enemy's reach, or attack while retreating from the enemy. They used their somewhat unorthodox skill set to toy with their foes. Fundamentally, dread knights weren't tanks; they were attackers. Considering Ranta's personality, he might have been more suited to that, too.

Still, they couldn't have Yume, with her light armor, be the second tank, and Haruhiro couldn't do it either. Merry, as the priest, and Shihoru, as the mage, were out of the question. By process of elimination, that left only Ranta.

*If we lose Ranta, the party would lose their second tank,* Haruhiro concluded. *We don't have a replacement, so that would hurt.*

*In that case, we could try to find another volunteer soldier, or something. Unlike priests—who have no shortage of groups looking for them—if we looked, we could probably find someone fairly quickly, is the sense I get. If we go to Kikkawa, with all his connections, he could probably find someone for us.*

*After all, Merry joined the party through Kikkawa's introduction. Things were a bit touchy at first, but she's gradually blended in with the rest of the group. He's excessively outgoing, and acts way too buddy-buddy with everyone, but Kikkawa's eye for people might not be that bad after all. At the very least, there've got to be plenty of warriors better than Ranta.*

*Maybe...it's an option, at any rate. It seems worth considering, if nothing else.*

Haruhiro could hear Moguzo snoring away.

*How about Ranta? Usually, he's the fastest to fall asleep. But, even now that I'm listening for it, I don't hear Ranta's distinctive snores.*

"Ranta," Haruhiro called, and got a response.

"...Yeah?"

"Listen."

"What?"

"There's something I should talk to you about."

"Hmph."

"But not here... I don't want to wake Moguzo. Can we go outside?"

"Fine with me."

The two of them went outside the lodging house. Haruhiro wondered just why that he had called Ranta out here.

*Do we have something to talk about? I sure don't want to talk to him. It's just...I feel like I have to tell him. Regardless of what I end up doing, if I planned it all out without him knowing and then suddenly one day threw him out, saying, "We don't need you anymore," that'd just be cruel. That'd be taking it too far. Even if it's Ranta.*

*Or maybe it's just that I don't want to act underhanded. Of course I don't want to. Of course not. If I'm just cutting Ranta loose, why should I have to plot in secret, like I'm getting my hands dirty somehow? It's not funny.*

"So, tell me," Ranta said.

Haruhiro crouched down, leaning against the building, and Ranta did the same.

"Hm?" Ranta demanded.

"How do I put this...? What do you think about it? The party, I mean," Haruhiro answered.

"The party's a party, isn't it? No more, no less."

"What's that mean? 'No more, no less'?"

"Have you got a problem with me? I think I'm playing my role pretty well."

"How...?"

"Well, I am, aren't I? I mean, just today, I proved I can take on one of them all by myself."

"Yeah, and if we'd all ganged up on it, it'd have been over in no time."

"Can you guarantee you'll always be able to do that? You can't, can you? If I can handle one of them on my own, it gives us some, what, breadth? Tactically? Something like that."

"...Even so..." Haruhiro held his forehead tightly in the palm of his hand. In his own way, is he thinking about things, too? *But, you know... even if he is...*

"I can't tell when you're doing that sort of thing," Haruhiro explained. "Not unless you tell me."

"What, do you want me to tell you every little thing I'm gonna do and what my intentions are beforehand or something?"

"I'm not saying you need to take it that far. I'm saying there are things I won't understand unless you tell me. You're already easy enough to...misunderstand, I guess you could say."

"I'll bet you don't think it's a misunderstanding at all." Ranta picked up a pebble and threw it. "It doesn't matter what I'm thinking. You've all come up with your own impressions of me, and you all judge me based on that."

"...Even if that's true, our impressions of you are built based on the things you've said and done."

"What, you're saying it's *my* fault?"

"Well, whose fault do you think it is?" The blood was rushing to Haruhiro's head. "Is it mine? Yume's? Is it Shihoru's? Moguzo's? Or Merry's?"

*I need to calm down,* thought Haruhiro. *I don't want to start a fight.*

Haruhiro sighed. "You're working in a group. There needs to be... what's it called...a willingness to cooperate? We need that."

"And you're saying I lack it?"

"Do you think you have it?"

"I don't."

"Oh..."

"Hey, we've all got our strengths and weaknesses. If I've got weaknesses, what about the rest of you? You don't have *any*? I'm the only bad one, and you're all a bunch of saints?" Ranta demanded.

"...No, that's not true," Haruhiro hesitated.

"What's my weakness?" Ranta asked. "That I'm selfish?"

"And loud and annoying?" Haruhiro added.

"Shut up, scumbag."

"You're foul-mouthed. Also, you're quick to blame others."

"Not everything can be entirely my fault. It's a joint responsibility, a joint responsibility. That's what it means to be in a party, you know!"

"You're always making pointless arguments like that," Haruhiro objected.

"It's not a pointless argument! It's a perfectly valid one!"

"If I keep on listing your faults, we'll be here all night," Haruhiro said.

"Then how about you, huh, Haruhiro? What are your faults?" Ranta snapped.

"I'm..." Haruhiro went quiet.

—*Faults.*

*My own faults.*

*It's not that nothing comes to mind. I've got them. In fact, it's harder to think of my strengths.*

"Why should I have to talk about that in front of you?" Haruhiro said finally.

"You're always bringing up my faults, but when it comes to yourself, you're gonna go quiet, huh? Yeah, I figured you would. That's how you people operate."

"How...*we* people operate?"

"Am I wrong?" Ranta demanded. "I'm an easy target, so you all attack me, and what comes of it? You get to build some sense of unity? You're all banding together, you know that?"

"No, we aren't really."

"Can you deny it? You can't, can you?"

"...It's not like we're all conspiring to attack you."

"Yeah, you don't have to conspire to do it. It's an unspoken agreement, isn't it? Basically, I'm your scapegoat for everything."

"I'm telling you, you've got a persecution complex."

"Do you seriously think that?" Ranta smirked sarcastically. "Well, it must be *nice* being you guys. Thanks to me, you're able to turn a blind eye to each other's faults. But, have I ever complained about that? I only said it now because you brought it up, Haruhiro. If you hadn't, I had no intention of ever bringing it up myself. I'm not interested in trying to be buddy-buddy with the rest of you. I couldn't stand playing at being friends like that. That's why, if you guys want to hate me, well, hate away. I'll gladly play the antagonist for you, or any other role you want. It doesn't bother me; we're a party, after all. I'll play my role. That's what it means to work in a group, doesn't it?"

Haruhiro tried to say something in response, but couldn't. He couldn't find the words.

Haruhiro had been trying to tell Ranta *Please, get out of our party.* That it was for the good of the party. Honestly, he hadn't been confident he could say it without hesitating. If he hadn't, he'd wanted to at least talk things over. *If you don't fix your bad tendencies, we can't work together anymore.* That was what he'd been thinking.

Had he been too one-sided about things? Were he and the others using Ranta as a scapegoat, like Ranta said?

*I don't think so,* he thought.

There were things about Ranta that deserved criticism. It was Ranta's own fault that everyone blamed him.

*We're not wrong. Ranta's wrong.*

If that was the case, shouldn't he cut Ranta loose after all? It'd make him feel better, at least. He could explain to everyone later. His comrades would probably support Haruhiro's decision.

He couldn't say for certain he wouldn't regret it, though. When the time came, the one to regret it most would probably be him. Because, as the one who had thought about it, come to a decision, and cut Ranta loose, he'd be carrying the heaviest burden.

*Why should it be me? Why only me?*

"I'm going to sleep." Ranta stood up and went into the lodging house.

Haruhiro couldn't move from his spot.

*There's a heavy weight in my stomach. I'm sick of this, I think. I don't want to deal with it anymore. I don't want to think. I'm just not suited for it. It's too much. Being a leader. I can't take responsibility. Help me, Manato. Yeah...I know. I can't turn to Manato for help with this anymore.*

"...It's so lonely," Haruhiro said out loud.

*I shouldn't have become the leader.*

*I don't have the capacity for it.*

## 6. Even If It's a Detour

*You know, humans sure are mysterious,* Haruhiro thought.

Even after all that agonizing—to the point that everything seemed like too much effort, and he felt he'd be happier if tomorrow just never came—after he went to sleep and woke up, he felt a little refreshed.

Ranta didn't seem any different than usual, so for now, things were the same as ever.

There was only one thing to do. Today, they'd go to the Cyrene Mines again. And if they were going, they had to make a good profit from it.

With that in mind, Haruhiro and the party dove into the Cyrene Mines, putting down lesser kobolds and low workers without any real risk as they steadily proceeded to the second level. They had turned back at this point yesterday, so today, their goal was the third level.

Haruhiro felt they weren't used to the kobolds enough yet, but compared to the day before, he could follow their movements and predict them, as well.

*This seems pretty workable...?* he thought. Although that sort of optimistic outlook could easily lead to a nasty fall.

The well came into sight. Beside it, there was a kobold. No.

"That's—a kobold...?"

Because he'd spotted what looked like an enemy in the distance, Haruhiro had everyone hold up while he went ahead to scout. And what he saw made him doubt his eyes.

*It's huge.*

*Could that be an elder? But...normal kobolds are about 150 cm tall, and elders are around 170, I've heard. Is that difference enough? Isn't that one even taller? That really big one is dragging around three smaller kobolds with it; it's one or two sizes bigger than the smaller ones.*

*Even those small ones, though, feel taller than the normal kobolds. They've got armor that looks like it's got high defensive power, they're wearing helmets, and they're carrying swords and round shields. If that guy's two sizes larger than them, is he two meters tall?*

*—Hold on, that guy's...*

"White and black..." Haruhiro murmured to himself. There was something white mixed in with its black fur, giving it a spotted appearance.

*My heart just skipped a beat. Oh, crap. It doesn't seem to have noticed me yet, though. If it notices me, I'm in serious trouble. It's scary. Way too scary. What's with that sword it has? It's probably a meter or two long. It's thick. Like a massive carving knife. If it gets a good hit in with that, it'd probably cut me clean in two. That weapon looks damn heavy, but it's carrying it like nothing. What monstrous strength.*

*Merry's party fought that thing? They were crazy,* Haruhiro thought, despite himself. *Yeah, they'd die. Of course they'd die.*

There was no comparing it to the armored goblin and hobgoblin that had been such formidable enemies for Haruhiro and his party. It was a completely different sort of thing. It was clearly powerful and dangerous.

Haruhiro turned back to where the others were. He couldn't see his own face, but his expression must have been terrible.

"...It was Death Spots," he said, dejected.

"Huh...?" Shihoru was at a loss or words.

"Muh!" burst out Moguzo. It seemed he was, too.

*Hold on, what does "muh" mean, anyway? What's "muh"?*

Perhaps Merry had anticipated this to some degree. She furrowed her brow, just giving a slight nod.

"It's Red Splotch, huh," Yume whispered.

"You mean Death Spots..." Haruhiro dutifully corrected her, which helped him to calm down a little. Haruhiro looked to Ranta.

"We've gotta do it," Ranta said, laughing. He probably thought he had a dauntless grin on his face, but he just looked like a moron.

*Well,* I *knew he'd say that,* Haruhiro thought.

"Okay. Fine, Ranta, go take him on alone. Do your best."

"...So that's how it's gonna be, huh? You've got no blood or tears, do you, pal?"

"Yeah, say whatever you want. So? What'll it be? You gonna go? Or not? Which is it? Choose fast."

"Looks like I've got no choice." Ranta rubbed the tip of his chin with his thumb. "I'll save it for next time. Though it just means Death Spots dies a little later, that's all."

"Yeah, yeah, good for you."

"You ought to say that to Death Spots. Because it's the one that had its life spared."

"You go tell it that yourself. I've got better things to do," Haruhiro retorted.

Haruhiro tried not to banter with Ranta any more after that. It seemed even Yume, who'd always been ready to tell off Ranta up until yesterday, had gotten completely sick of it, too. Haruhiro noticed only he and Ranta were talking, which almost made it seem like they got along.

*I really don't like that,* he thought as they headed for a different well. There were five wells that went down to the third level from the second level, so it wasn't much of an inconvenience.

At this well, there was no sign of any person—no, any kobold—around. Haruhiro tried peeking into the well, but there didn't seem to be anything down below, either. Though, that said, there was a limit to how much he could see from above.

"I'll go down first," he told the party. "If there's no trouble, I'll call, so come down."

"What'll you do if there's trouble?" Yume asked, blinking.

"Well...in that case, I'll call, so come save me."

Yume grinned. "Sure thing."

*That's kind of soothing.* Haruhiro returned Yume's smile. "Well, I'm off, then."

There were rope ladders going down the well. The ropes looked old, but they didn't seem like they'd break under a person's weight.

Even if he wasn't much of one, Haruhiro was still a thief, so he slid down one of the rope ladders quickly. When he reached the third level and turned around, some kobolds were waiting.

"Oh, hello there," he said.

"Grrrrrrr..."

"—Wait, this isn't the time to be saying hello!" Haruhiro leapt back as one of the kobolds came at him.

*This kobold's big! Not as big as Death Spots, though. An elder, huh?*

The elder was wearing chain mail and armed with a single-edged sword. Two normal kobolds were with it, similarly dressed.

"B-Below! Here! Enemies! Whoa! Help...!" Haruhiro's speech ended up fragmented.

Haruhiro ran around trying to get away from the elder and normal kobolds. However, he couldn't leave the bottom of the well. Until his comrades came down, he had to stay here.

But there were three of them. If it had been one, he might have been fine, but racing against three opponents was pretty hard on him. Wherever he ran, there was a kobold. If he turned around, there was a kobold. If he leapt to the side, there was a kobold. Kobold, kobold, kobold. It was like a kobold festival.

"Urkh...!"

Haruhiro tried to slip past the elder's blade, but he took a deep cut to his cheek. He couldn't really feel the pain, but knowing he'd been hit frightened him.

*I can't tell the enemies' positions, if my comrades are coming, anything. If I see a kobold, I run. That's all I can do. Not moving away from the bottom of the well isn't going to be possible. I don't have that kind of leeway. There's no way I do!*

"Take that!" Ranta's voice bellowed.

*Have I ever been so glad to hear Ranta's voice? I don't think so. No, definitely not.*

Ranta came straight down and, even though he probably shouldn't have, he attacked the elder.

*This is Ranta we're talking about, so I doubt there's any deep thought behind it. Probably it was the closest when he came down, and it was the biggest, so it caught his eye first, or something like that. The reason he was the first to come help probably wasn't that he wanted to save a comrade who's in a pinch and acted immediately. He's fundamentally thoughtless, but that lets him act on the spur of the moment. It's a weakness that's also a strength—I guess...?*

"Urgh!" Moguzo grunted.

"Haru-kun...!" Yume shouted.

"Ohm, rel, ect, vel, darsh...!" Shihoru chanted.

"Haru!" And Merry appeared.

One after another they came down, and soon, Haruhiro had regained his composure. At first, Ranta had been keeping the elder busy, but now he'd swapped out with Moguzo. Ranta and Yume took one each: Kobold A and Kobold B.

"Haru, are you injured...?!" Merry asked.

Haruhiro softly rubbed his cheek. There was a jolt of pain, but so long as he didn't touch it, it was fine. "I'm fine! It can wait!"

Haruhiro went to support Yume, taking aim at Kobold B's back.

*At the same time, I need to take stock of the situation around us.*

*—I can't imagine I have the ability or qualifications for it, but, technically, I'm the leader.*

*Ranta, well, he's doing all right. He uses Exhaust to retreat quickly, then looks for a chance to use Avoid, and, if he can put some distance between them, he attacks with Hatred or Anger from outside the enemy's reach. I feel like he's moving around too much, but maybe that's just how a dread knight fights. Though, when Ranta does it, you can't help but get annoyed at him for running all over the place.*

*Moguzo and the elder are evenly matched, I guess. Moguzo hasn't been able to strike a fatal blow yet, and the elder's blade occasionally manages to hit him, but—No, that's not it. I'm pretty sure he's letting it hit him.*

*Moguzo wears plate armor, so a light cut won't deal any damage to him at all. It'll scratch his armor, that's all. The strong slashes he dodges or blocks with his bastard sword, while the weak ones he lets through to be stopped by his armor. Moguzo's able to distinguish between them like that.*

"You're no hobgob...!" Moguzo suddenly bellowed, stepping in closer.

Moguzo's bastard sword collided with the elder's sword. Their blades locked.

"Hungh...!" Moguzo shouted.

Quickly, Moguzo wound his sword around his opponent's blade, slashing at the elder's face with Wind.

The elder took a cut to its cheek like Haruhiro had and jumped back in a hurry. Moguzo roared and followed up with another strike. "Hungh!"

A shiver ran down Haruhiro's spine.

*It's amazing how stable Moguzo is in battle. And, on top of that—it really does help that Ranta can handle one of them. He looks like he's able to fight with more composure than yesterday, too. Is it experience?*

Because Ranta had pushed himself the day before, maybe he had found some trick or rhythm to it.

*In anything, there are things you just don't know until you've tried it for yourself,* Haruhiro thought. *Approaching everything carefully, only doing things you're sure you can do. If you just keep choosing the safe plan like that, you either don't move forward, or if you do, you move slowly. For instance, if I acted as the party's helmsman, and everyone just did as I said, they'd probably only move forward a little at a time.*

*—Do we need Ranta...? I have trouble seeing it that way.*

*Or is it that I don't want to think that?*

*Though, Manato probably recognized that we need Ranta. That said, it wasn't that Manato liked Ranta all that much. If it wasn't about liking or disliking him, did he decide based on something else? It felt like Ranta didn't oppose Manato quite so often. And when Manato died, Ranta seemed to take it pretty hard...in his own way.*

*What's different between me and Manato? What is it...?*

Well, of course, there were lots of things. Especially when it came to their abilities, there was just too great a difference.

Manato had been able to get along with Ranta, while Haruhiro couldn't. So what was different? Was it okay to write it off as a matter of ability, or aptitude?

Suddenly, Haruhiro saw a line.

It was dim, but he saw a faintly shining line.

It connected Haruhiro's dagger and a point on the kobold's back. It wasn't a straight or even a curved line. It turned and twisted.

Somehow, he knew that he just needed to follow that line.

He wished he could see the line all the time, but that just wasn't how it worked. He didn't even see it one time in a hundred. No, the odds were even lower than that.

Whenever Haruhiro encountered an enemy, the first thing he tried to do was get behind them. Actually, it wasn't just the first thing—he always tried to.

Then, every second—perhaps more often than that—he would ceaselessly look for that moment. If you were to count the number of times he'd done it, it was thousands, perhaps more by now.

Because Haruhiro felt like it was all that he had. Fighting an enemy head-on was impossible for him. He'd felt that keenly after his first fights against the pit rats and the mud goblin. No matter what enemy he faced, in a straight-up, fair contest of strength, he didn't have the power to win.

That was why, unfair as it might be, he hit them in their backs where they were the most vulnerable.

He felt it was pathetic, but not completely pathetic. After all, this was a matter of life and death.

Both sides were serious. It didn't get any more deadly serious than this. There was no way it was going to be easy, so he'd resort to anything he had to. That was something he'd learned from Manato.

When he could see the line, he had to keep his breathing steady. If he held his breath, or inhaled or exhaled in the wrong way, the line would disappear in an instant. He couldn't bend his knees and lower his center of gravity, either. He couldn't put too much strength into his wrist, elbow, or shoulder.

He didn't have time to think about what would happen if he missed this chance. He needed to act immediately.

Or, rather, by the time he saw the line, his body was already in motion. That's what it felt like. If his body didn't go into motion automatically, he would never succeed. Rather than him choosing to follow the line, it might be more accurate to say that by the time he noticed, he was already following it.

This time, it worked.

Haruhiro's body moved smoothly, his dagger easily entering the kobold's back. The kobold spewed out its last breath and collapsed.

"Huh?" Yume blinked, staring at it in blank amazement.

"Yume, next!" Haruhiro shouted.

Yume nodded quickly. "Y-yeah! Yume was surprised! Sorry 'bout that!"

"—Ohm, rel, ect, vel, darsh...!" Shihoru chanted, casting the Shadow Beat spell.

*Vwong.* The shadow elemental, which looked like a black ball of seaweed, flew forth.

The elder noticed and tried to avoid it, but it grazed its arm. The elder was wearing chain mail, so it probably didn't do any damage. However, Shadow Beat didn't use heat, or impact, or electricity: it used vibration.

The elder's right shoulder trembled with a *bwong.* For one instant, the elder stopped moving.

"Thanks...!" In that moment, Moguzo attacked with the Thanks Slash. The elder still managed to block with its sword, but it wasn't in the right position. The elder's sword was pushed back by Moguzo's bastard sword, drifting to the side.

"Hungh!" Moguzo immediately followed up with a strike from another angle, burying his bastard sword in the elder's flank. The elder tried to counterattack, but before it could, Moguzo kicked it to the ground, and when the elder landed on its backside, he brought his bastard sword down on its head.

"Yeah!" Haruhiro pumped his arm a bit in celebration. There was just one kobold left.

Ranta pulled back with Exhaust again, probably hoping to lure the kobold in. However, it obviously saw through it. The kobold didn't move up.

When it didn't, Ranta leapt forward to unleash his Hatred. But the kobold had expected that, too, and it sidestepped him to the right. That meant the kobold had managed to circle around to the side of Ranta. Barking, it swung down its sword.

"Whoa...?!" Throwing himself to the ground, Ranta narrowly evaded the kobold's attack. A close call.

"Ranta...!" Haruhiro was about to race forward.

"Don't come!" Ranta shouted, rising to one knee and deflecting the kobold's sword. "I've still got this! I'm gonna take this guy down! I've gotta kill him with my own two hands and earn my vice!"

"...What, weren't you doing it to give us more tactical breadth?"

"It's both! Exhaust...!" Ranta zoomed backwards from his half-crouching position. "—Whoa?! That was a new Exhaust! Maybe, did I just discover an original skill of my own?!"

"It didn't look any different than usual," Yume said coldly.

"...Yeah," Shihoru agreed.

"That's right," Merry concurred.

"Ha ha ha..." Even Moguzo's laughter sounded dry.

"You goddamn maggots!" Ranta shouted.

While throwing some hateful invective their way, Ranta went to attack the kobold.

*Let's just leave him to it,* Haruhiro thought. *Well, until it looks like he's going to die, at least.*

_Grimgar of Fantasy and Ash_

# 7. Leave It To Sensei

Elder talismans were nice.

They were earrings, nose rings, and occasionally necklaces, too. Regardless of what they were, they almost always had a jewel in them worth more than 5 silver. There was even a time when a single gem sold for 40 silver.

The second level of the Cyrene Mines was home to the low workers, but the third level was home to a slightly higher class known as kobold workers.

The elders on the third level seemed to be their supervisors and so, they were called foremen. Foremen traveled with two to three followers in tow, and while these followers were built like the workers, they were properly armed. Haruhiro and the party were targeting both these kinds of kobolds.

How strong these groups were depended on the foreman. Its strength was an important factor, but how capable it was at commanding its followers could affect the feel of the battle greatly.

If the foreman came right up front, things would be surprisingly easy. However, when the foreman drew back, siccing its followers on them, things could get pretty hard.

Like humans, they generally focused on doing something about the enemies in front of them. It wasn't that this was a trait of theirs, or anything complicated like that; if you had an enemy in front of you, but you looked around for other enemies, what would happen? Well, you'd get killed. That's why they had no other choice but to do things that way. For reasons of practicality, they had no choice but to focus on defeating the enemies in front of them.

That said, sometimes their priorities could change.

For instance, if an ally was in trouble, it was possible they'd choose to expose themselves to the enemy they were facing to go save them.

Also, they could be ordered to do so.

Haruhiro couldn't give unreasonable orders to his comrades, but a foreman could. Even if a follower was fighting Moguzo or Ranta, the foreman might gesture and bark for them to go after Shihoru or Merry instead.

When that happened, whether it was out of bravery, obedience, or even a dog-like adherence to the pack hierarchy, they'd follow the foreman's orders at great risk to their own lives.

If they got past Moguzo and Ranta, the others would be in real trouble. In particular, Shihoru, as the party mage, couldn't fight in melee combat, so everyone had to cover her. Whenever that happened, they broke formation, and the battle bogged down.

However, if they could just eliminate the foreman, its followers were no match for them. As far as Haruhiro was concerned, all they needed to do was focus their strategy on taking down or otherwise neutralizing the foreman as quickly as possible.

At the moment, there was always one foreman and two or three followers. The fact that there was no variation in their enemies' composition was working in their favor.

The hunting here was simple, but good.

It also felt good that they had the fourth and fifth levels to look forward to. When the appropriate time came, they would naturally start to consider taking the next step up, a thought which gave their morale a boost.

After ten days of coming to the Cyrene Mines' third level, they had built up some money, so they decided they'd each learn some new skills or magic. They wanted to broaden their options in battle, and being able to do more things gave them a firm sense that they were growing.

Haruhiro decided to pay forty silver coins to Barbara-sensei and learn the Spider technique from her.

"Okay, let's do this right away, Old Cat," she said.

Skill training was done in a room in the thieves' guild in Alterna's West Town called the "Poisoning Room." It sounded more dangerous and terrifying than was probably necessary, but most rooms in the thieves' guild had names like that.

Incidentally, the Poisoning Room was fairly big, but it had no windows. The only light came from a chandelier with candles that could be raised and lowered from the ceiling. It wasn't a bright room by any stretch of the imagination. Even in the middle of the day, if the candles weren't lit, it was pitch black. It was a creepy room.

Barbara-sensei was wearing highly revealing clothes, like always, and today, she had a black scarf wrapped around the lower half of her face. Her long hair hid one of her eyes as well, making her look kind of scary.

"...Okay," Haruhiro said. "Thank you for your instruction."

"You seem awfully stiff," Barbara-sensei told him. "The only part of you that should be stiff right now is your crotch."

"Uh, no, I'm not stiff there, eith—"

Before he could finish getting the words out, Barbara-sensei was behind him. When he tried to turn to face her, she put him in a full nelson. Was that what it was called?

Barbara-sensei did more than just pin both his arms; she also wrapped her legs around his.

*I can't move!* he thought.

On top of that, Barbara-sensei had her knife at Haruhiro's throat.

"Spider...is a skill where you pin your opponent from behind in an instant, then deliver a fatal blow. If I were doing this for real, I'd have slit your throat wide open. Even if I hadn't had my knife, snapping your neck would have done it. If I hadn't wanted to kill you, just neutralize you—" Barbara moved the point of her knife down from Haruhiro's neck, stopping it at his crotch. "—I could cut here. It's quite effective on men, I assure you."

"...I'm sure it is. Uh, um... could you get away from me now, maybe...?"

"Hm? Oh, right, you've never known a woman. You're not used to this, huh? So, if I were to do *this*..." Barbara blew in his ear.

"Wha—?!" Haruhiro tried to throw his head back, but Barbara was holding him still, so he couldn't. "—Leave my ear alone, okay?!"

"I just *blew* in it a little, that's all."

"I'm kind of weak there, you could say..." he mumbled.

"You're hopeless. Okay, then—"

"Huh?"

Haruhiro had no idea what happened next. His body flew through the air, spinning once, then he landed on his back, knocking the wind out of him.

Barbara-sensei looked down at Haruhiro. "Once I have you grappled like that, there are all sorts of things I can do. First, you're going to thoroughly experience my Spider. We'll go until I have you coughing up blood."

"...Are you sure I won't die?"

"If you die, you'll never know, so why worry? Well, I wouldn't want No-Life King's curse to bring you back as a zombie, so I'll have you cremated at least. Don't worry."

*What if I really do get killed?* Haruhiro thought. *I dunno what other mentors are like, but Barbara-sensei's been like this from day one. But, technically, she hasn't killed me off yet, and I've learned the skills she teaches me. I can trust her... I think.*

A moment later, he thought, —*Is this okay? Really?*

After three hours of experiencing the many variations of Barbara-sensei's Spider, Haruhiro couldn't even stand.

"What's wrong? You're acting slovenly, Old Cat."

"...I'm sorry," he managed.

"If you can't get up anymore, there's no helping it. Let's take a break." After saying that, Barbara-sensei sat on Haruhiro's belly.

"Oof."

"Deal with it. Even when you rest, you should be training. Sit-ups. Do sit-ups. Or maybe you'd like some training on how to endure torture?"

"I'm going to die, seriously."

"Now, now, I'm holding back, aren't I? So far, I've only killed a handful of people in training, I'll have you know."

"You've actually killed people, then...?"

"It was a joke. Why would I kill my precious source of income? Now then, it's about to get heavier."

"Urkh..."

Barbara-sensei lifted one leg, and the amount of weight on Haruhiro increased accordingly. At this point, he needed to strain his stomach muscles a fair bit just to bear it.

"Now, let's double it," Barbara-sensei said.

"Oh...!"

This time, she raised both legs. Barbara's full weight pressed down on Haruhiro's belly.

*How is this a break? I can't rest like this.*

"Well, let's make small talk," she said.

"I...can't..."

"Just do it, idiot!"

*It's an unreasonable demand, but that's nothing new. Besides, if I don't do as Barbara-sensei demands, things will only get worse for me.*

"U-um, let's see... S-small talk..."

"A short story would do, too."

"I-I don't have anything like that."

"What a boring man you are. *This* is why women won't sleep with you."

"I-I can't...deny that."

"You've got women in your party, I'm sure. How many?"

"Th-three."

"Make at least one of them yours," Barbara-sensei told him.

"Though gobbling *all* of them up is the way to go."

"No, I couldn't do that."

"Because it would cause trouble in the party if that stuff was going on?"

"I-I wouldn't know. I don't have any experience..."

"A little trouble makes things fun. Ah, I remember those days. When I was in your position, I tried hooking up with my party leader. Then, I started two-timing on him with the guy who was our mage. Then, I had a fling with the leader of another party after he confessed his love to me, and when everyone found out, the party fell apart... So many memories."

"...I don't know that it fell apart so much as you broke it up."

"It feels like youth, doesn't it?" Barbara-sensei reminisced.

"It feels like blind passion, too..."

"Nice one," she said.

"Urgh!"

Barbara-sensei kept both legs raised, grinding her butt against him. It was unbearably painful. Though if he were to thrash around and try to throw her off, there was no telling what she might do, so he had to bear it.

*Still, Sensei's sense of balance is pretty amazing,* he admitted to himself.

"This is the only time to do it," she told him. "You're sixteen, aren't you? When you're sixteen, there are men, and there are women. Really, this is the only time that's true. Once this time goes by, it never comes back. If there's a girl who interests you, you'd better do something about it now, or someone else might snatch her up. I say 'might,' but if there's a woman you want to do it with, there are other men thinking the same thing, so she's *going* to get snatched up. If you start regretting it after seeing her and some other guy fondling one another, it'll be too late."

"W-well, I don't have anyone," Haruhiro said. "I don't have a girl I'm interested in."

"You *really* don't?" Barbara-sensei asked.

"...Huh?"

"Old Cat. You tend to try to play it safe. You don't want to rock the boat with your party, so you're unconsciously setting those feelings aside, aren't you?"

"Th-that's not..."

"From my experience, men fall for the women who are close to them. Probably that's just how men are. Though women can be the same way."

*The women close to me.*

*Yume.*

*Shihoru.*

*And Merry.*

*I don't dislike any of them.*

*With Yume, I do think her goofiness is kind of cute, sometimes. And we did hug that one time. But that was just because of the situation. Sure, I can still feel it now, or remember how it felt, but if I ask myself whether I have those sorts of feelings for her, I don't think so... Probably.*

*Shihoru... She actually has rather big breasts, I guess.* Since that was the first thing that he thought about her, Haruhiro started to worry that he was some sort of savage. *I'm pretty awful, aren't I?*

*Besides, it'd be awkward with Shihoru. She seemed to be...in love with Manato, after all. No, it's not just that she seemed to be... I'm pretty*

*sure she was. For me to do something with Shihoru—yeah, no. I couldn't even consider it.*

*Well, what about Merry, then? As for her...she's off-limits in another way, I think. I mean, Merry is just too beautiful. And she's got a great figure, too.*

For Haruhiro, who was the plainest of the plain, she was a little— no, very—unapproachable. *She's a comrade, though, so I do need to close the distance between us a little,* he realized.

*Before, when we asked who in the party was her type, Merry answered Moguzo. She's probably not too hung up on looks, herself.* However, if Moguzo was her type, then did Haruhiro have no chance? *Well, not that my chances matter. I've never felt that way about Merry. I haven't... right?*

*I do wish she'd smile more. If I can, I want to make Merry smile more. Given how beautiful she is, if I could see Merry with a broad grin on her face, I'm sure she'd look stunning. It'd be a heartwarming sight.*

*But, that's not love, it's something else—right...?*

"...Um, Sensei?" he asked.

"What, Old Cat?"

"I'd like some advice...or to ask you something, rather..."

"Of course! It's about women, right?"

"No, it isn't..."

"Oh, ho! Dodging the subject, are you? You good-for-nothing."

"I don't have time for it. I don't have the time to think about that stuff. I've got bigger worries. Honestly..."

Changing the subject, Haruhiro spoke to Barbara-sensei about the line he saw sometimes in battle.

The lower half of Barbara-sensei's face was hidden by her scarf, so it was hard to read her expression. But, somehow, it felt like she was listening seriously. As he was talking, she rested her legs back on the floor.

"—I see. That's not a bad sign," she said.

"A sign...?"

"However, don't misunderstand. It's nothing special."

"No, I don't know what there is to misunderstand. I mean, I don't have any clue what it is..."

"You sure are a dull one," she said. "In the end, you're just an old cat."

"...Am I dull? Well, I certainly don't think I'm sharp."

"You're dull. Still, despite that, your instincts aren't bad. That line you saw is something anyone who's gained some experience will have seen once or twice—or felt it, rather. That might be the more correct way to describe it."

"For me, it's been more than once or twice. It's not all the time, or even once a day, though."

"Sometimes it's like that. Well, it's wildly different for each of us."

"How about you, Sensei...?"

Barbara-sensei shrugged. "Sometimes I see it, sometimes I don't. It's not something you can see by focusing, after all."

"When I do see it, things go ridiculously well," Haruhiro said. "With Backstab, that is."

"But you know you can't rely on it, don't you?"

"...Yeah. There's no guarantee it will happen. It's like a fluke."

"There you have it. You need to improve your skills. Your stamina, too."

"*Augh...!*"

Barbara-sensei lifted both legs again. He couldn't see because of the scarf, but she was probably grinning devilishly.

"If you're able to say you don't have time for it, you've got a long way to go," she said. "Build up enough stamina so that you can kill five or six orcs and then still go a round or two with a woman. If you do that, you'll naturally develop a desire for women, and you'll put some more effort into your love life. If you aren't a *real* old cat, that is."

"I'm fine with being an old cat."

"Don't get salty with me!"

"*Yowch?!*"

"Whoops...sorry, put a little too much strength into it there."

"...*Ohhh...*" Haruhiro came close to fainting in agony. Barbara-sensei had struck him in the crotch.

*If I keep training here, am I eventually going to end up impotent?* he wondered.

# 8. Unsuitable

Having learned Spider without incident—okay, with some incident—Haruhiro and his party resumed their daily trips to the Cyrene Mines.

Ranta had apparently learned a dread knight spell known as Dread Terror. It used the menace of the dark god Skullhell to terrify his opponent, robbing them of the ability to think properly.

*Depending on how he uses it, it sounds like it'd be useful,* Haruhiro thought. *Now, if only Ranta would use it cleverly.*

Moguzo had learned Fast Thrust and Back Thrust together as a set. Fast Thrust was a one-handed thrust, and from what he told them, it had a fairly long range. Back Thrust was a thrust used when backing away.

*Ranta often backs away using Exhaust to lure the enemy in so he can hit them with Avoid, so it's probably something like a plainer version of that,* Haruhiro surmised.

Shihoru had learned the Shadow Bond spell. This attached a shadow elemental to the ground, and when someone stepped on it, it'd stick to them and keep them from moving. She could only have one active at a time, and a strong opponent could tear free, but she said she could maintain it for up to twenty-five seconds.

Unlike Sleepy Shadow, it didn't have the limitation of being ineffective on an agitated target.

*It's the perfect spell for Shihoru, since her personality leans more towards assisting than attacking,* Haruhiro thought.

Yume had learned a skill called Star Piercer. It was basically a knife throw, but by throwing a variety of different blades thousands of times, she'd really gotten the knack of it. Yume had procured herself a short knife to use with Star Piercer, as well.

Or, as she told it: "Yume, she didn't know what kinda knives'd be good, y'know, and so when she asked Master which kind're the best, y'know, Master took her to the market and he said 'This one, and this one' and he picked them out for her, and he said 'You can have just one,' and he offered to buy one for her, and that made Yume so happy, y'know, but Yume still bought it for herself."

*It seems Yume's master in the hunters' guild is rather fond of her,* Haruhiro thought. *I can sort of understand why.*

As for Merry, she'd learned a light magic spell, Blame. It was an attack spell that used the light of Lumiaris to punish enemies. Its range was short, and it didn't inflict much damage, but it numbed those it hit, and for a short time, they'd move sluggishly.

*Probably she plans to use it when she wants to support Moguzo and the others on the front line without moving up,* Haruhiro thought.

With these new skills, the party's overall capabilities had definitely increased. In particular, Shihoru's Shadow Bond was tremendously powerful, as they discovered on the third level of the Cyrene Mines.

"That's amazing, Shihoru! You can even stop an elder with it!" Haruhiro cheered in admiration.

One of the more troublesome types of foremen—the ones who led their followers from behind—was being held still by Shihoru's Shadow Bond. Even though it was just being held in place, and should have still been able to give orders to its followers, it seemed to be panicking.

"Now's our chance! Get its followers!" Haruhiro shouted.

As if to say he knew that without Haruhiro telling him, Ranta pointed at Follower A with his left hand. "Come, darkness! O, Skullhell! Bring an infinite horror upon those who resist! Dread Terror...!"

Something like a sort of purple haze engulfed Follower A. When it inhaled that haze, Follower A yelped and then—came swinging at Ranta.

"—Whuh?!" Ranta blocked Follower A's sword with his own, but his opponent didn't stop. Metal sounded on metal as it swung its sword frantically. It was a fierce assault that defied all common sense.

Ranta cried "Whoa?! Wha?! Wh-what is this?!" He was barely managing to hang on. "This isn't what they said it'd be like...?!"

"...Well, it *does* seem like it's been robbed of the ability to think properly," Haruhiro commented.

*Yep, Ranta's still Ranta all right. Anyone who expects anything from him is only setting themselves up to look like a fool.*

*There are three followers in total. Let's see the other two. Moguzo's taking Follower B, and Yume's taking Follower C—oh, but Merry's stepped in already.*

"O Light, may Lumiaris' divine protection be upon you...Blame!"

The one Moguzo was facing, Follower B, was showered in light, causing its entire body to twitch.

"Thanks!"

Moguzo's deadly Thanks Slash cut down Follower B, allowing him to immediately go aid Yume. The way he didn't force himself to use his newly acquired skills was typical of the easy-going Moguzo.

"...Guess there's nothing else for it." Haruhiro decided to go help Ranta.

As he tried to take up a position behind its back—

*Oh!* He noticed something.

Ranta's Dread Terror probably hadn't frightened Follower A, but instead whipped it into a death-crazed counterattack. From Ranta's perspective, it was a horrible failure, but not from Haruhiro's. Follower A couldn't think of anything but brutally murdering Ranta, so Haruhiro wasn't even on its radar.

*If it's like this, I can easily get behind it. Do I go for a Backstab? No—*

"Since I have the opportunity, I'll use Spider!" Haruhiro shouted.

Haruhiro grappled Follower A. For now, he had gotten used to instantly locking both arms in position. He wasn't so good at the legs yet, but just robbing it of the free movement of its arms gave Spider a high chance of succeeding.

Haruhiro jammed his dagger into the underside of Follower A's jaw, slashing it hard. He then immediately backed away. Follower A wasn't dead yet, so if he held on too long, he exposed himself to the possibility of an unexpected counterattack, but that wasn't all...

"Rarrrgh...!" Ranta slashed at it. Ranta hit the already-dying Follower A with the hardest blow he could muster, then followed it up with a stab through the heart to finish it. "Mwahahaha! Vice!

Viiiiice...!"

"—That was dangerous! What if you'd hit me?!" Haruhiro shouted.

"If *you* die, I get another vice! Hurrah!"

*He's such an ass. Though I already knew that. If I accept that's just how he is, it doesn't make me mad. Okay, no, it does. It really makes me mad. But I can give up and accept it...maybe?*

"There! Hah...!" Yume shouted.

Once Yume had cornered Follower C using Brush Clearer and Diagonal Cross, Moguzo bellowed "Thanks...!" and finished it with a Rage Blow.

"Quick, get the foreman!" Haruhiro shouted. Whenever he said something blatantly obvious like this, he felt embarrassed.

*But when I shout, it focuses the entire party's minds on the same thing, which helps build momentum, so there's a reason for it. I don't have time to feel embarrassed.*

Haruhiro and the others ganged up on the foreman that was finally able to move again. Of course, the foreman was desperate, too, and so, it put up a fierce resistance.

From their experience, Haruhiro and the others had learned the best way to deal with an opponent like that. Rather than surround it on all four sides, attacking it blindly, they waited for it to attack, and then defended. Everyone but the person defending would attack. This would continue until their enemy exhausted itself.

*In the end*, Haruhiro thought later, *after it was all over, we managed to take down the foreman without anyone getting injured. Ranta's contribution was as dubious as ever, but I think it's fair to call this a perfect victory.*

"I'd say we're done with the third level, don't you think?" Ranta said. "Opponents like these just aren't enough of a challenge. Let's move up to the next stage already."

"You're doing it again..." Haruhiro wasn't overly enthusiastic about the idea, but once they finished off another foreman with four followers and reached the well down to the fourth level, the thought *Heading down might be an option, I guess,* did cross Haruhiro's mind.

*We've gotten into a good groove today,* he thought. *Maybe I should go along with it.*

On the other hand, *I'm scared of getting too far ahead of ourselves. Isn't it times like this when we usually get tripped up?*

"Hmm..." He stood in front of the well, deep in thought. He stayed like that for probably five minutes.

"How long are you gonna agonize over this?!" Ranta shouted.

*This time, Ranta has a point. I'm agonizing over it too much, even by my standards. What does everyone think of their leader being like this? Moguzo and Shihoru look worried. Yume's staring off into space. Merry seems pensive. Ranta's the only one who's snapped, but it's still not okay. I need to be able to make decisions when it's time to. Okay.*

*I've decided.*

"...Let's do it tomorrow," he said.

"Huh?!" Ranta immediately came at Haruhiro.

*I'd expected this, but—ugh, he's such a pain.*

"It's fine, isn't it?" Haruhiro asked. "What's the problem? We'll each prepare ourselves, then tomorrow we'll challenge ourselves to—"

"Prepare myself? I'm already prepared, and I have been for a long time!"

"If you're the only one who's prepared, then it doesn't mean a thing!"

"You *say* I'm the only one, but, really, it's just that you're not ready! You chicken!"

*Ahh. Not good, not good. I'm about ready to blow my top.* Haruhiro closed his eyes and took a deep breath. If he got emotional and engaged in a verbal slugging match, no good would come of it.

*Control myself. I have to control myself. But why should I have to control myself for Ranta? This is all Ranta's fault. Damn you, Ranta.*

Haruhiro opened his eyes, making sure not to meet Ranta's. If he looked at Ranta's face, he was sure he'd be too mad to act rationally.

"Tomorrow, we'll go down to the fourth level. Today, level three is as deep as we go. Ranta, you're opposed to that, right? What about the rest of you?"

Everyone but Ranta answered that they were fine with it.

*I'm sure Ranta's going to put up a fight...* was what Haruhiro thought, but surprisingly Ranta didn't, which left him feeling let down. *I just don't get him. What's with him?*

After that, they circled the third level, taking down two foremen and four followers without injury. They were able to return to Alterna safely, and they had earned a decent amount.

The party ate dinner together, then went to Sherry's Tavern for a drink. While they were drinking, Kikkawa came up to them, and they had a good time swapping stories. Ranta and Kikkawa seemed to get along. They put their arms around one another's shoulders, making a little—no, a large—ruckus.

*Is it a matter of compatibility?* wondered Haruhiro. When he thought about it, Haruhiro argued with Ranta more than anyone. Maybe they were just a poor match for one another.

After leaving the tavern with the rest of the party and walking a short ways, Haruhiro came up with an appropriate-sounding excuse and headed back on his own.

Merry was on the first floor of the tavern at the end of the counter. When Haruhiro approached, Merry noticed and turned to face him.

*What'll I do if she's not happy to see me?* wondered Haruhiro, scared for a moment. *Maybe I am a chicken, like Ranta said. Well, I'm definitely not brave, that's for sure.*

Fortunately, his worries were in vain. It may have been slight, but Merry smiled.

"Is something up?" she asked.

"Uh... Nothing really. Mind if I join you?"

"Go right ahead."

Haruhiro sat down next to Merry. Merry was having mead again so Haruhiro ordered the same.

*Lately, I've been eating and drinking a lot more of things I like. Maybe it's time to consider graduating from that shabby volunteer soldier lodging house, too.*

"Where do you live, Merry? Ah..." When he heard how the words sounded as he said them, he panicked a bit. "No, I mean, it's not that I want to know where you live, I was thinking it's about time we stopped living in the lodging house, you know... So, I was wondering what sort of place you live in, as, you know, a point of reference, or something..."

"I just live in an ordinary rental building on Flower Garden Street," Merry said, unperturbed. "It's a place that only takes female tenants. I've been renting a room there all this time."

"Oh. I see."

*I look like an idiot for being so overly conscious,* Haruhiro thought. *If there's a hole around here somewhere, I want to crawl into it. I won't, though. My brow's kinda sweaty.*

Haruhiro brought his palm to his forehead, casually wiping the sweat away. "Oh, that sounds nice. After all, I'm sure you'd rather not have a guy in the room next to yours."

"If they're leaving the lodging house, would you like me to introduce the place to Yume and Shihoru?"

"Sure. I think they'd like that. Though, it's not like it's a sure thing we're moving out yet. Actually, no one's even brought it up... We've gotten used to the place, and it's fine in its own way, I suppose. Sort of. It can be inconvenient in a lot of ways, though."

"The lodging house, huh." Merry lowered her eyes, taking a sip of mead. "That brings back memories."

*When Merry was staying in that rundown lodging house, I'm sure she must still have been with her original party. With her comrades that are gone now.*

"There are more people there now, at the lodging house." Haruhiro said with a laugh. Even he wasn't sure why; it was a meaningless laugh. "You know, the new volunteer soldier trainees are there. Their rooms are far away from ours, and I've only said hello to a few of them so far, though."

"What are they like?" she asked.

"It didn't seem like there was anyone like Renji, I guess? But...they don't seem as unreliable as we are, either."

"I don't think you need to be so self-deprecating."

"Do I seem that way?" he asked.

"A little."

"I am, aren't I...?" Haruhiro wanted to hold his head in his hands, but he stopped at just scratching his hair. "That's not good, huh? I wish I could be more proud, but, somehow, that's just not who I am as a person."

"A confident Haru." Merry smiled a little with her eyes. "You're right; it doesn't suit you."

"I know, right? No, I guess I shouldn't be so readily agreeing here, either."

"Maybe you're thinking about it too seriously?" she suggested.

"Huh? I am? You think? Seriously? Am I?"

"You handle Ranta seriously, too. That's why you two fight."

"Ahh. You could be right there. I wish I could let things slide better..."

"When you try to do things right, it just makes it harder, doesn't it? I think you don't need to take everything so seriously. When you *really* need to, you'll have no choice but to get serious, anyway."

"Be less serious, huh...?"

Haruhiro had a hard time believing he was a serious person to begin with. *But when it comes to leading the party, I've been agonizing a lot about the right way to handle things. It's true that, in my own way, I've been thinking seriously.*

*It's probably because I'm not suited to it. If I were... If I had the aptitude for it... I'm sure I wouldn't be agonizing over it so much.*

*I always end up thinking the same thing in the end. Honestly, if someone could take my place, I wish they would.*

*When I'm talking with her like this, Merry seems overwhelmingly more suitable for it. Can't she take the job? Not that I could say that. I could never bring myself to say something so pathetic.*

"You know, there's something I've been wanting to ask you, Merry," Haruhiro ventured.

"What?" she asked.

"It's about the Cyrene Mines."

"Oh..." Merry said, then closed her mouth.

From here on, Haruhiro and the others would be going down to the fourth and fifth levels. Like Merry and her party once had.

If they did, someday, the time was sure to come. Merry would once again have to enter the place where she had lost her friends.

Haruhiro had experienced it himself, so he knew: That was hard. Very hard.

Every time he had gone to scout on the armored gob and hobgob, there'd been a sickening feeling in Haruhiro's chest. More than sadness or anger; it had been an unbearable feeling.

Ever since that day, Haruhiro and the others had almost never returned to the spot where Manato had breathed his last. They wanted to forget the place existed at all.

"Merry, I'm worried that you might not want to do this. Going to the Cyrene Mines. You're not forcing yourself, are you? You don't look like you are, but..."

"It doesn't feel...pleasant," Merry said, as if chewing on each word. "I can't feel good there. Not now, and probably not ever."

"...Of course not."

"Still, I need to get over it." Merry shook her head. "No, I want to get over it. If I don't, I feel like I can't move forward. But I'm sure I can't get over it all by myself. If I have to borrow strength from someone else...I want it to be you guys. Because you said you're my comrades."

For some reason, Haruhiro's eyes felt hot. No, not for 'some reason.' It was because he was happy.

Merry was relying on Haruhiro and the others. She was

recognizing them as her comrades. Believing in them. And now, she'd talked about it with him. More than anything, that made Haruhiro unbearably happy.

"I may be troubling you," she said, "but..."

*The way Merry added that makes her seem so sweet, and I want to hug her—is one audacious thing I will definitely not be doing! I couldn't do it. Besides, Merry probably doesn't want me to.*

*But I did think she was cute just now.*

*Because I want to protect her? Then again, the question of whether I can protect her or not, that's doubtful.*

"It's no trouble, okay?" Haruhiro gave her a smile. *I hope I look even somewhat reliable, but it's probably just not who I am. At the very least, I hope I can reassure Merry even a little.*

"It's no trouble," he repeated. "I'll lend you as much of my strength as you want. I can't do what I can't do, but if I can do it—Wait, it's because I say things like this that I can't keep up appearances."

"Haru, aren't you fine that way?" she said gently.

"Am I?" he asked.

"Thank you," Merry said in a tiny voice, as if she were embarrassed.

*Whoa, this isn't good,* Haruhiro realized. *I felt like I was going to fall for Merry there.*

*I won't, though.*

*After all, I'm not good enough for her.*

## 9. Let Go of Jealousy

*I really don't think I'm suited to be the leader,* Haruhiro thought the next morning. *I don't have the personality, or the ability for it. I could try to work on that, but it'd be hard.*

Even so, after talking to Merry the night before, Haruhiro had firmed up his resolve. He was going to do his best to be a leader. He might not be able to be a good leader, but he'd try to become a passable one, at least.

And so, as he'd declared they would the day before, they'd come to the fourth level of the Cyrene Mines—

"Look. See. Look, look," Yume said, reaching out over a fence and pointing at something on the other side of it. "Those critters're pretty darned cute, aren't they?"

Right away, Ranta disagreed with her, shouting, "How is *that* supposed to be cute?!"

This was the one time Haruhiro had to agree with Ranta.

The creatures waddling around on the other side of the fence looked like pigs. However, they also had a rat-like appearance to them.

If you blew a rat up to pig-size, then shaved it bald, it might have looked like this.

They didn't know what the kobolds called these things, but volunteer soldiers apparently called them pigrats. It was a fitting name.

There were a large number of fenced enclosures, and pigrats were being kept in them. No, not just pigrats.

"Yume thinks they're cute, though," Yume said. "Oh, but, those ones over there are cute, too!" She raced over to another enclosure. "...Uwah, now that Yume's takin' a closer look, maybe not."

"...Those creatures..." Shihoru shrunk back, trying not to go near the enclosures. The only reason she was still looking at the creatures was out of morbid curiosity. "...They're obviously gross...I think. *Really* gross..."

"Y-yeah..." Moguzo nodded.

"You know..." Haruhiro said, taking one glance at the other creatures that weren't pigrats. The way they looked, he wouldn't have wanted to look at them directly. "...these things are messed up. I dunno how else to put it: they're messed up. I feel like I'm looking at something I really shouldn't look at."

"Ah..." Merry winced a bit. "I might understand what you mean. Kind of."

The other creatures had no arms or legs. No tail, either. They weren't long and slim, they were long and fat. They looked like someone had pulled the limbs and tail off a pig and then stretched it out. They were pretty scary. They were called pigworms, apparently. Of course, that was just the name that volunteer soldiers called them by.

"Hmm," Ranta said. He reached out with his sword to poke one of the pigworms.

"Hey." Haruhiro stopped him right away. "Cut that out, Ranta."

"Huh? Shove off. I was just trying to do it. I wouldn't have done it for real."

"If you were trying to do it, how does it follow that you weren't going to do it for real?" No sooner had the words left Haruhiro's mouth than he regretted them. It was best to just let whatever Ranta said go, but now he'd gone and given him a serious response.

"In my mind, it follows just fine," Ranta said.

"Yeah, whatever," Haruhiro muttered.

"It totally follows. Do you get it?"

"I get it, I get it."

"Fine, explain it to me then," Ranta demanded.

"In your mind, it follows just fine," Haruhiro said.

"You just repeated exactly what I said!"

Ignoring Ranta's ranting, Haruhiro took another peek at the pigworm herd. The way they crawled by twisting their bodies around was probably going to haunt his nightmares. "That's what kobolds eat, huh..."

The fourth level of the Cyrene Mines was known as "the farm."

This part of it was more of a ranch than a farm, but they grew darkshrooms, holly-fern, and lightflowers—the plants that grew around the mine and provided a light source, unusual plants that could grow without sunlight.

Kobolds were living creatures. If they didn't eat, they'd die. It seemed that, aside from the lesser kobolds on the first level, they rarely ventured outside, so they needed to be self-sufficient inside the mine.

The ore veins had long since been exhausted and there was a lot of open space on the fourth level, so this was where they had their food production center.

"Hide," Merry said suddenly, making a pressing-downward gesture with her hand.

Haruhiro, Shihoru, Moguzo and Ranta immediately ducked down, but Yume remained standing all on her own.

"Huh? What's up?"

"—Now's not the time!" Haruhiro hurriedly grabbed Yume by the arm, pulling her down to a crouch.

He'd only meant to pull her down that far, but with a "Whah," Yume landed on her butt. "Owwie..."

"S-sorry. Wait, no, actually—" Haruhiro brought a finger to his lips and said, "Shh." He mouthed the words, *Be quiet.* Yume seemed to understand and nodded.

Haruhiro and the others clung close to the fence, staying put for around three minutes maybe.

Ranta poked his head up over the fence. "—Hmm. They're gone. I think."

"You think...?" Haruhiro slowly poked his head halfway above the fence, looking around the area. There was one elder in the distance, but it had its back to them. It seemed to be going away. "...There's one there. Let's hide a bit longer."

However, another minute later, when he checked again, another elder was coming in their direction.

"Oh, crap!"

"Oh, come on," Ranta sighed. "How long do we have to hide? Maybe we oughta just kill it?"

"Hmm..." Haruhiro looked at Merry.

Merry shook her head. "I don't think we should. From the fourth level down, things are different than on the first three. If we don't finish it off in an instant, they'll be all over us in no time."

Ranta snorted derisively. "Well, we've just gotta finish it in an instant, then."

"Don't make it sound so simple," Haruhiro said exasperatedly.

"We might be able to do it," Shihoru said. "With my magic."

"Ah," Haruhiro opened his eyes wide. "That's right. Sleepy Shadow."

"Yeah. But...if I fail, we'll be in danger... Maybe we shouldn't..."

"Listen, you," Ranta said with an exasperated look on his face that was endlessly aggravating. "If you worry about what'll happen if you fail, you can't even drink water. Because water could always be poisoned. You get what I'm saying? I'll bet you do. Yeah?"

*If you're going to make an analogy, at least try to come up with a better one,* Haruhiro wanted to say, but he let it go. If he was going to lead this party, letting things go was one of the skills he needed to develop.

"Shihoru," he said. "You don't have to do it if you don't feel confident, but if you're feeling up to it, why not try? I mean, you did come up with the idea, after all."

*Shihoru's so passive, it's unusual for her to offer an idea herself. I want to encourage her,* he thought.

Shihoru looked down for some time before finally raising her face. "...Can I try it?"

Nobody objected.

After luring the elder within Sleepy Shadow's twenty-meter range, Shihoru poked her face and staff out from behind the fence and started chanting. "Ohm, rel, ect, krom, darsh."

The shadow elemental that launched from the tip of her staff

wasn't as fast as when she cast Shadow Beat. But it was quiet. It flew silently, catching the elder.

*It got its face,* Haruhiro observed.

The shadow elemental entered the elder's body through its nose, ears, and mouth. The elder immediately began to stagger, falling to the ground not long after.

"Okay!" Haruhiro gave the order, and everyone charged out.

*Attacking a sleeping elder is kind of cowardly, isn't it? But that's not something I've time to think about right now. We have to hurry and finish it off quickly.*

Ranta was the one to strike the killing blow. He was always extremely fast at times like this. "Gwahaha! One easy vice! All right, people! Take its stuff!"

"What're you giving the orders for?" Haruhiro argued with him without thinking. *Oops, I'm not supposed to do that. Let it go. Let it go.*

Unlike the elders of the third level, the elders here wore armor with iron plates, carried iron whips, and wore iron rings around their waists. This one's talisman was a necklace that shone with a bluish silver color. It looked like it was valuable.

"That was easy-peasy, huh?" Yume said. "Yume kinda feels just a teensy bit sorry for the elder, though. You were great, Shihoru. Gettin' it with a pew, pew of your magic like that."

"Y-yeah," Moguzo agreed. "It was easy thanks to you, Shihoru-san."

With Yume and Moguzo praising her, Shihoru said "...I-it was no big deal..." in a humble tone.

"No, really," Haruhiro turned to Shihoru, giving her a thumbs-up. "You did perfect. I mean it. If we find an enemy on its own that hasn't noticed us yet, we know this method will work for sure now."

"I was the one who got the kill, you know?" Ranta broke in.

*Okay, just let it go.*

"This elder..." Merry looked down at the elder's corpse, making the sign of the hexagram. "It wouldn't be a good idea to leave the body here."

"Ahh," Haruhiro looked to the fence. "Why don't we shove it in there? Inside the fence."

Now that it had been stripped of its stuff, Moguzo and Haruhiro worked together to dump the elder's corpse into the enclosure with the pigrats. Ranta ought to have helped, too, but Haruhiro decided it wasn't worth the hassle to say anything.

Soon after they finished, something horrifying happened.

"Whoa..." Haruhiro said out loud.

The pigrats oinked loudly, gathering around the dead elder's corpse and then...*No way, they wouldn't eat it, would they...?*

Yes, way. They ate it. They went into a feeding frenzy, fighting each other over the carcass.

Yume mumbled, "It's the food chain..." or something like that, but was that really the issue? That wasn't, was it?

"...Ohhh," Shihoru clutched her staff, looking like she was ready to faint at any moment.

Merry looked nauseous, covering her hand with her mouth. Moguzo stood there in a daze.

"Actually, this is convenient for us, isn't it?" Ranta was the only one with a strange grin on his face as he watched the ghastly sight... but... "No matter how many of them we kill, the pigrats'll dispose of the bodies for us. Though these pigrats'll eventually end up in a kobold's belly, so that's kind of gross when you think about it. Well, we're not the ones who'll be cannibals here, so it's not our problem. Ha ha ha ha ha..."

"Your legs, they're shaking, you know?" Haruhiro pointed out.

Ranta stammered, "H-huhhh?" trying to sound intimidating, but he wasn't scary at all. He looked at bit pale. "I-I'm not shaking. H-how am I shaking? Y-you're the one that's shaking, and I just look like I'm shaking because you're shaking, see?"

"What do you mean, 'see'?"

"Shut up! See is... See is, oh, I know, the 'C' in cruelty!"

"If it's making you sick, you don't have to force yourself to watch..."

"Y-you moron," Ranta said. "It's not making me sick, okay? This is nothing. Actually, I love this kind of stuff. When you're a dread knight, erotic and grotesque stuff just comes with the territory."

"Grotesque, maybe. Erotic, on the other hand... I'm just not seeing how that's relevant here."

"I want it to be relevant! I'm a guy, okay?!"

Still, it seemed wrong getting rid of the bodies this way, and because the pigrats were in such a frenzy over the unexpected feast, a number of elders rushed over, forcing the party to hide again. Hiding wasn't going to be enough, though. They needed to get away, or they'd be in trouble.

However, if they were to try to move, even with the high fences of the pigrat and pigworm enclosures making it easy to hide, there were a lot more elders patrolling the area now. On the other hand, the darkshroom, holly-fern, and lightflower farm had no fences, making it easy to see them, and there were a good number of low workers and workers out in the fields.

Haruhiro and the others ended up sneaking their way to a desolate corner of the fourth level where there were just empty enclosures with no creatures in them yet.

"...Maybe it's going to be hard to work on the fourth level?" Haruhiro asked, leaning back against one of the fences.

Merry thought for a moment then said, "The conditions here might be bad. We also—Ah..."

Merry stopped short with an *oops* expression on her face. She might have been worried that by referring to her previous comrades as "we," she might offend her current comrades, Haruhiro and the others. Haruhiro was about to tell her not to worry about that, but someone beat him to the punch.

"What? You don't need to be so touchy about that." It was Ranta, of all people. "Do we look so small and petty? If anything, we're big-hearted. And, me, I'm wild, too. Don't fall in love with me, okay?"

"Yeah. I *won't*," Merry responded immediately.

"Trip!" When Ranta did his exaggerated facefaulting routine, Merry chuckled a little.

Haruhiro fought a twinge of annoyance... *Huh?* he thought. *Am I feeling jealous, maybe? Jealous of Ranta, at that...?*

Haruhiro cleared his throat, bringing his mind back to the task at hand. "—Well, how about the fifth level, then?"

Merry responded cautiously. "It's better than the fourth level, probably."

"Mhm, mhm," Yume nodded lightly.

"...In that case," Shihoru said hesitantly, "should we go down...to the fifth level?"

Moguzo exhaled deeply through his nose.

Ranta grinned. "It's decided, then."

## 10. You're Supposed to be Lame

When they descended the well's rope ladder to level five, the first thing that struck Haruhiro was—*It's hot.*

It had been chilly, if anything, in the first four levels, but things were different here. The temperature was clearly higher.

The reason for that soon became apparent. The tunnels of the fifth level were lined with furnaces, large and small. The ore they mined was brought here to be smelted. The fifth level was the refinery.

Of course, that meant there were kobold workers busily at work at the furnaces that were operational. That said, not all of the furnaces were currently operating. Some furnaces weren't turned on, and there was what looked like a place for the workers to take breaks.

Some places were full of kobolds, while others were quieter. Every once in a while, an elder or worker would wander along. There were good places where that happened, too, which were perfect for volunteer soldiers.

Merry knew some of those good areas, so Haruhiro and the others decided to take up positions around one.

It was at the end of a tunnel, but it wasn't a dead end; for some reason, the path looped back around in a circle. It was a long way from any of the operational furnaces, but the workers' break area and elders' watch post weren't far from it. Maybe they were using it as a place to go for a walk to relax, because apparently, kobolds showed up here once in a while.

Haruhiro and the others lay in wait for them.

*...They're not coming,* he thought.

"Ngrargh!" Losing his patience, Ranta let out a weird cry.

Yume made a big show of sighing. "If waitin's so hard for ya, why don't ya go take a nap or somethin'?"

"Yeah, and when I do, I bet you're planning to take the opportunity to abandon me here!" Ranta snarled.

"Good guess."

"Yeah, I'm a good guesser, Tiny Tits. I know how you think. I see right through you!"

"Don't call them tiny!" Yume screamed.

"When you say it like that, what kind of idiot wouldn't do it? They're tiny, tiny, tiny, tiny, tiny, tiny, tiny, tiny, tiny, tiny, tiny, tiny, *tiiiiiny!*"

"Murrrrrgh..."

"Y-Yume..." Shihoru patted Yume on the back. "Um, I don't think your breasts are tiny..."

"Oooh," Yume moaned. "Shihoru, it's no comfort hearin' that from someone who has really big breasts."

"Huh...? I-I'm just fat... But, I'm sorry..."

"Nuh-uh. Yume's the one who oughta be sorry. Don't you worry about it. You didn't make your breasts grow that big, Shihoru, and

Yume didn't make Yume's breasts small, either. Besides, y'know, Yume's a hunter, so she uses a bow every once in a loooong while. When she does that, if her breasts were too big, she kind of thinks they might get in the way."

"...Well...you could be right, yeah..."

"See? Bein' a hunter may have been Yume's callin' in life..."

"Oh, come on, *that's* your reason...?" Ranta snorted.

Haruhiro didn't entirely disagree with Ranta's sentiment, but he decided not to touch the subject.

*Just let it go. Let it go. Let it go.*

While he was sitting there building experience points to get his Let It Go skill up to the next level, Haruhiro sensed something coming.

The vast majority of the fifth level was quite noisy, but around this out-of-the-way spot, it was quiet. This was a mining tunnel, so sounds echoed, too.

*I hear footsteps coming. Probably a kobold.*

Haruhiro raised a hand, pointing into the distance. Then, he stuck his thumb out and gave the thumbs-down sign. In the time since they started frequenting the Cyrene Mines, they'd settled on this as their *enemy incoming, prepare for battle* sign.

Yume readied an arrow, closing her eyes and taking a deep breath. Moguzo with his bastard sword, Ranta his longsword, Shihoru her staff, and Haruhiro with his dagger each took up fighting stances. Merry was holding her priest's staff tightly, as well.

Haruhiro breathed. *I see it. It's an elder.*

Yume opened her eyes. She had activated the Quick-eye skill, which used special eye exercises and self-hypnosis to improve her ability to see at a distance, even improving her kinetic vision on top of that.

She fired.

"Yipe!"

She scored a hit on the elder's face.

Another one came in from behind the elder that was writhing in agony.

*That's another elder. We've got two elders. The wounded Elder A, and the unharmed Elder B.*

"Moguzo, take the unharmed one...!" Haruhiro began.

Moguzo was already rushing towards it as Haruhiro gave the order.

Ranta attacked Elder A. "I'll kill you!" he shouted.

Yume set down her bow and drew her machete.

Shihoru chanted a spell. "Ohm, rel, ect, vel, darsh...!"

It was Shadow Beat. A shadow elemental that looked like a blob of black seaweed launched from the tip of Shihoru's staff.

Elder B blocked Moguzo's bastard sword with its wide-bladed sword. In that instant, the shadow elemental struck it in the belly. Its entire body was stricken with convulsions.

"Hunngh!" Moguzo pushed past Elder B's sword, slamming his bastard sword into its head—but it suddenly dodged aside, preventing him from splitting its head wide open. Elder B leapt backwards with the side of its head slashed open.

"Take that!" Ranta stabbed Elder A, knocking it down, then buried his longsword in its chest.

When Haruhiro and Yume went to assist Moguzo, Elder B turned and ran.

"Don't let it get away!" Merry shouted.

"Yeppers!" Yume shifted her machete to her left hand, drawing a throwing knife with her right. It was her Star Piercer skill.

The throwing knife stabbed into Elder B just below the shoulder, but it didn't fall. It was still running away.

Moguzo plodded after it, swinging his sword down with a cry of "Ugah!" but he couldn't reach it.

"Leave this to me!" Haruhiro shouted. With his quick legs, he left Yume behind and passed Moguzo as he rushed ahead.

Elder B had its back to Haruhiro. It was fleeing in desperation, so it wasn't watching its back at all. It was wounded, so it was a little unsteady on its feet, too. Haruhiro could catch up like this.

"Spider!"

Wrestling with it, he swiftly slit its throat with his dagger then immediately backed away.

Elder B flailed about for a while before falling to the ground dead.

Haruhiro breathed a sigh of relief. "...I did it."

"Got my vice!" came the barbaric cry of joy from Ranta.

*Sounds like Elder A's dead, too.*

"You know..." Haruhiro couldn't help but smile a little. *It may not have been clean, but, you know.... I think that wasn't half bad.*

*We didn't overburden Merry, the priest, and we each were able to use our own styles to end it quickly. That's what I'd call "teamwork."*

"That was pretty good just now, wasn't it?" he said. "I think it felt good, don't you?"

"M-me too," Moguzo nodded his helmeted head repeatedly. "That's what I was thinking. Just vaguely, though."

"Y'know..." Yume flared her nostrils, slapping her upper right arm with her left hand. "When Yume's arrow hit and when her Star Pierce went off, she felt sorry for the poor elder, but, Yume, she felt so good."

Shihoru was grinning broadly. "...We had a good tempo going...I feel. Like, it occurred to me naturally who would do what next...and then they actually did what I expected, something like that..."

"Yes," Merry smiled. "I think that was good."

"It's all thanks to me, though! Truly, what's mine is mine!" Ranta shouted.

*...Ranta's still the same as ever though, huh?*

Now, he could have let it go, but this time, Haruhiro just couldn't. "Yeah, of course what's yours is yours," he snapped. "If it weren't yours, whose else's would it be?"

"W-wait! I got it wrong! I didn't mean to say what's mine is mine... uh, the world! The world is mine! I just screwed it up a bit! I wanted to say the world is mine!"

"Yeah, whatever. Good for you."

"You don't think it's good at all, huh?! Not with the way you're saying it!"

"No, no, I do. Congratulations."

"Thanks!" Ranta kicked the ground. "Wait, why should I have to thank Haruhiro?!"

Normally everything Ranta did irritated him, but despite himself, Haruhiro found the way Ranta was acting kind of funny, so he laughed just a little. With a relaxed mood hanging in the air, Haruhiro was about to go collect the loot when he noticed something seemed off and looked around the area.

"What's—" Merry began.

*—the matter?* was probably the rest of what Merry had tried to say. But before she could finish speaking, she must've spotted the same

thing Haruhiro did.

From around the bend in the tunnel, something was poking its head out. That something was a kobold. It must have noticed Haruhiro and Merry looking at it, because the kobold pulled its head back.

"Oh?" Ranta pulled the talisman off Elder A's body. "This guy had some nice stuff. Hey, get a look at this, guys, it's—"

"Wait," Haruhiro raised his hand for Ranta to be quiet, glancing to Merry. "What do you think?"

"Huh?" Ranta cocked his head to the side. "About what?"

"Somethin' up?" Yume was crouching on one knee next to Elder B's corpse.

Shihoru, who was crouching next to her, looked at Haruhiro, blinking. "...Huh? Wh-what is it...?"

"Nngh..." Moguzo sat down.

Merry brought a finger to her chin, pensively. "...What do I think? Well—"

*Awoooooooooooooooooooooooooooooooooooo...*

They heard a voice. It was similar to a dog's howl. Similar? It sounded exactly the same. But, of course, it wasn't a dog doing the howling. It was a kobold. They didn't know if it was an elder or a worker, but it was the kobold they had just seen.

"H-hey..." Ranta swallowed his spit, brushing his mouth with one hand. "Wh-what? W-was that a bad sign, just now...?"

Merry nodded, her eyes wide. She was clearly losing her cool. "This is bad. That was—"

*Awooooooooooooooooooooooooooooooooooo!*
*Awooooooooooooooooooooooooooooooooooo!*

149

*Awoooooooooooooooooooooooooooooooooooooooo!*
*Awoooooooooooooooooooooooooooooooooooooooooo!*
There was a chain of howls.

It wasn't just one voice. After the first kobold howled, other kobolds who had heard it howled, too, and then other kobolds who heard them howled—now, there were several kobolds howling.

"L-let's run!" Haruhiro made a snap decision. He grabbed Yume and Shihoru by the arms. "G-get up! Come on!" he cried, hauling them to their feet.

*Run. That's right. We have to run away. But, which direction?* For a moment, he wasn't sure. *Calm down. It's all the same, isn't it? That's right. This is a circular tunnel. No matter which way we go, it's the same. But what comes after that? The layout of the fifth level is complex. Do I know the route? Can we make it back to a well and the fourth level without getting lost? I'm not bad at remembering my way. But I'm not good at it, either. Probably, I can manage—I think. I'm not that confident. Man, I'm really shaken up.*

"Come on...!" Merry took off running.

*Right. Merry knows. I just have to stick with Merry. Merry knows this place.*

"L-let's go, everyone!" Haruhiro shouted, saying something nobody needed to be told. Then he chased after Merry. He ran for a little while, then looked back. Once he confirmed everyone was keeping up...

*This is no good at all,* he thought to himself. *I'm supposed to be the leader, but I'm just scrambling to save myself. For a moment there, I forgot my comrades completely. That's pathetic, and I'm embarrassed to admit it. Yume and Shihoru have totally lost their heads. I need to reassure them. Reassure them...?*

*In this situation...? How?*

"It's okay!" Haruhiro shouted, then almost bit his tongue, thinking immediately, *How is this okay?*

At the very least, Haruhiro wasn't okay. He was panicking so hard it'd have been laughable, but he really didn't have the time to laugh.

He couldn't run facing backwards, so he turned back around and kept running.

*It's shaking. My field of vision is shaking. It's shaking so hard, I have to wonder why it's shaking so much. My heart's pounding. Is this what they mean when people say their heart raced so fast they thought it'd escape from their mouth?*

Soon they were out of the circular tunnel. There was a guard post not far away. Also, a break area. These areas had been vacant when they came. Not anymore. Kobolds that looked like workers came out of the break area. They kept piling out.

"Oh, crap! Oh, crap! Oh, crap! Oh, crap...!" Haruhiro blurted out the words without intending to. His head was filled with nothing but "Oh, crap"s and "What now?"s.

Merry slowed her pace. Haruhiro followed suit and dropped his speed, as well.

*Oh, yeah. That's right. There're kobolds in the direction we're headed. If we keep going, we'll charge right into a pack of them. But, even if we turn back, there's nowhere to run. We have to charge in. But, if Merry's the one to do it...*

"M-Moguzo!" Haruhiro turned back. "M-move up front! You be the vanguard! Use War Cry...!"

"Umph!" Moguzo's voice had a tinge of desperation, but he raced past Haruhiro and Merry with heavy steps.

There were ten kobolds, possibly more, and they swarmed at Moguzo with what looked like fire pokers.

"Fungh...!" Moguzo came to a sudden stop. Several of the fire pokers battered against him. Moguzo was undeterred, planting both feet firmly on the ground and roaring.

"Ruohhhhhhhhhhhngh...!"

It was the warrior skill, War Cry. He let out an incredible shout using a special vocalization technique to intimidate the enemy. If someone heard it without having time to prepare—whether they were human, another race, or a monster—the first thing they were bound to do was cower.

One kobold leapt into the air. Another's legs gave out underneath it. Still more clutched their heads and backed away.

"Now!" Moguzo bellowed in a voice that sounded strangely manly.

Haruhiro moved his legs with everything he had. "Quick...!"

"Wahooooo!" Ranta let out a strange cry.

Merry was running alongside Haruhiro. Where was Yume? And Shihoru? Haruhiro glanced behind him. They were there. Both of them.

"R-run! Run! Run...!" he shouted.

*It's really lame that that's the only thing I can say.*

Haruhiro and Merry soon caught up to Moguzo. That was partially because Moguzo was slow, but also because he was weighed down by his armor, too. It was clanking and rattling like crazy. Haruhiro wondered if he should move up front.

*No, I shouldn't. It won't work. There's a kobold up ahead of us. Kobolds, rather. Several of them. I dunno how many.*

"I-I can't do it again right away!" Moguzo said between heaving breaths, pumping his legs as hard as he could.

*He can't use War Cry repeatedly,* Haruhiro realized. *What now?*

Haruhiro shouted, "W-we'll have to charge into them...!" His voice sounded shrill.

*Charge into them? Is that gonna be okay? I mean, do we have any other choice? I wish I could vent my frustration at someone right about now. Not that we have the time for it.*

"Oh! Oh! Ohhhhh....!" Moguzo's battle cries sounded pathetic.

A kobold and Moguzo collided with one another. There was an awful clattering sound. Then, three or four kobolds jumped in, piling on Moguzo.

He fell.

He fell over.

Moguzo tripped, fell over, and rolled. He used the momentum to get right back up on his feet.

"...Muh?"

Moguzo himself didn't seem to know how things turned out that way, as he stood there looking confused.

"Don't stop, Moguzo!" Haruhiro shouted.

Moguzo responded, "Foh?! Fohngh!" and started running again.

*What is "fohngh" supposed to mean? What is "fohngh"?* Haruhiro wondered.

"Make a right...!" Merry yelled out directions.

"Get away from me, you mutt!" He could hear Ranta's voice, too.

"Eek!" screamed Shihoru.

Haruhiro turned back to look. A kobold had grabbed the hem of Shihoru's robe.

"Hi-yah!" Yume slashed into the kobold's wrist with her machete. That chopped its hand clean off, keeping it from pulling Shihoru to the ground.

"Ungh! Ungh!" Moguzo swung his bastard sword around, scattering kobolds as he ran.

"Ah...!" Merry used her priest's staff to knock back a kobold that came at her.

*Whoa,* Haruhiro realized. *I'm not doing anything here. I'm just running away. Well, not that there's anything I can do but run.*

*How did it come to this? Things were going so well. That's right. Things were going well. Things felt great, and we had a good atmosphere going, too. Everyone was in high spirits. Did we get carried away, maybe...? No, it didn't get that far. We were about to, though. We were one step away from it.*

*Did we let our guards down?*

*I can't deny it.*

*The fact is, we didn't notice the kobold. Actually, by the time we did notice, it was too late. 'Too late'? Really?*

Haruhiro hadn't done anything, but maybe he could've. He couldn't say for sure that there was nothing he could've done.

*In the end, we were having too good a time.*

*When we push our luck, nothing good ever comes of it. When we lost Manato, it was because our belief that we could handle things came back to bite us. And yet, here we are, repeating the same mistake. We couldn't apply the lesson Manato paid with his life to teach us.*

"What the hell am I doing...?" he muttered.

*I'm the worst. Just terrible. I'm hopeless. Still, blaming myself isn't going to improve the situation. I don't think anything I do is going to turn this situation around.*

*It's no good. We can't get away. It's over. This is the end.*

*I mean, there are so many kobolds. There's an incredible number of kobolds here. If we go straight, there are kobolds in front of us and behind. If we turn, there are kobolds ahead of us there, too. There's nothing but kobolds. Where are we?*

Haruhiro had no clue where they were. It was all he could do to keep following Merry.

He could see Moguzo getting slower and slower. But, if he passed him, Haruhiro would be the vanguard.

*I can't handle that. I just can't. I can't be the vanguard. I don't think I can do it.*

Moguzo's wheezing. He's pretty winded. But he's still swinging his bastard sword around and running. Or trying to run, rather. Moguzo is desperately doing the best that he can for us.

*—I'm sorry. Sorry, Moguzo.* Haruhiro wanted to cry. *What am I saying I can't do it for? Even if I can't, I have to try. No matter how little, I have to buy Moguzo time to rest, or he's going to drop. Without Moguzo, there's no way we can escape.*

"Moguzo, I'll move up to the front!" he shouted.

*I'm scared.*

*I want to cry.*

*Damn it all!*

"Uwahhhhhhhhhhhhhhhhhhhhhhhhhhhhhhhhhhhhhh...!" Haruhiro raced past Moguzo, planting a jumping kick on the kobold that came at him.

*Oh, man, there are kobolds everywhere, nothing but kobolds, I'm amazed Moguzo managed this, this is scary, man, no way, I can't do this,*

*I'll die, uwahhhhhh!*

*I'm in pain, so I've probably been hit or cut somewhere, but I'm not sure where it was. I don't really have a good grasp of how I'm pushing these kobolds down or out of the way, either. It's like I'm going by instinct? Something like that? Actually, am I even moving forward? I wonder. For now, there's just one thing I'm completely sure of.*

The kobold in front of him, probably an elder, lifted up its sword, taking a hard swing at Haruhiro's head. For some reason, that scene seemed to freeze for Haruhiro.

He couldn't hear a thing.

It was strangely silent.

Somewhere, in a place that seemed familiar, yet unfamiliar at the same time, a room of some sort, he saw himself sitting in a chair.

*—What am I doing there?*

In another place, he saw himself surrounded by people who seemed familiar, yet unfamiliar. He was smiling.

*This time, I'm riding in some sort of vehicle. It looks like I'm going somewhere. There are other people besides me in the vehicle. Who are they? I know them...is what it feels like. But I don't understand. Not who those people are.*

*I'm crouched down in front of some big box full of light. There's someone standing next to me. A woman with her hair in a bob.*

—Choco.

That's what Haruhiro called the woman.

*Choco.*

*Who...?*

*I don't know. I don't know any Choco. But—*

*I feel...like I do know her.*

*Who...is she?*

*Where did we meet?*

*Did we meet somewhere?*

*At that place I saw just now...where was that...?*

*Choco. Hey, Choco. Who are you? Do you know me? Where was I? When? At some point—When I was in that place, did I know you...?*

*I don't know.*

*I can't remember.*

*—No.*

*That's not it. When I try to remember, the memory vanishes. Choco's face. Her appearance. But, Choco. That name is the one thing I remember. That one thing...didn't vanish.*

*But, you know...it doesn't mean anything. I'm going to die now, anyway.*

*You know, for some reason, the kobolds are moving really slowly, but they aren't stopped like they were before. They're moving. And yet, I can't move. I can't avoid them. I'm not wearing a helmet like Moguzo, so if that sword hits me in the head, I'm not gonna make it. I'll die...I think.*

*Could this be, you know? My life flashing before my eyes?*

*In that case, I really am going to die.*

*Choco, it looks like I'm going to die.*

*I wish I could've met you.*

*I only know your name, but I wish I could've met you.*

*But, it looks like that's not going to be possible.*

*I'll try to fight it. To dodge. Somehow. I don't feel the least bit confident that I can, though.*

*I mean, they're suddenly getting faster.*

The kobold's sword was coming. It was coming down. Haruhiro

raised his arm. He tried to block it somehow.

*I don't think I'll make it.*

"Anger...!"

*I don't think I made it.*

If Ranta hadn't leapt in and stabbed the kobold in the gullet, Haruhiro's head would've been cracked open for sure.

"Take that! Ranta-sama's coming through...!"

*I'm amazed he can still move like that.*

Ranta swung his longsword. He spun his body around, swinging the longsword with it. Then, he suddenly turned around. "Exhaust...!"

"Wha...?!" Haruhiro was caught by surprise.

It was a hip attack. Ranta used Exhaust to back up at high speed, not so much body-checking as butt-checking the kobold that was there and sending it flying. "Wahahahaha! I'm awesome...!"

"Thanks...!" Without missing a beat, Moguzo took down one of the kobolds with a rage blow while Merry used Smash with her priest's staff to knock over another kobold.

Yume went "Yah, yah, yah, yah...!" forcing a kobold back with her machete which Shihoru then struck with her staff.

"—There!" she shouted.

"Haruhiro!" Ranta deflected one kobold's fire poker with his helmet, stabbing it through the belly with his longsword. "You're weak, so be careful, you idiot! If you go and die on us, too—it'd be a problem!"

"...I *know* that!" Haruhiro snapped.

*You're the last person I wanted to hear that from.*

*Ranta.*

*You, you're the one person I never want to hear that from—but I can't blame you for saying it.*

*I'd totally given up. I was close to just accepting it. That's not good enough. I'm the leader. Yes, I'm incompetent. Yes, I'm weak. But even if I'm weak, I can still choose not to give up. Calm down. Even if I calm down, it's pointless. But even if it's pointless, I have to do it. I can't let myself be dispirited.*

*Are the kobolds my enemy here?*

*No.*

*The enemy is my weak self.*

"Merry! How far to the well...?!" Haruhiro shouted.

"A little further!"

"Okay! Hang in there, everyone! Let's stick closer to the walls! If you get into trouble, put your back to the wall! Being attacked from three sides is better than four! Ranta, you be the vanguard! Moguzo, move back! Yume and Merry, to the sides! Shihoru, don't push yourself! Let's move forward little by little!" Haruhiro shouted.

*There isn't a one of us who's unharmed. All of us are banged up all over. Still, we haven't lost heart.*

Haruhiro had come close to giving in once, but he was fine now.

When he looked closer, the circle of kobolds around them wasn't that thick. It wasn't as though there was a circle ten to twenty kobolds deep around Haruhiro and the others. There were a lot of them, yes, but they were poorly organized. They didn't move in unison, and when the party fought back, they'd get scared and run away.

Maybe because the kobolds had the overwhelming numerical advantage, they weren't taking it seriously. They weren't playing around, of course, but rather than surrounding Haruhiro and the others with the intent to kill, it was more like they were jeering at them and chasing them around.

Of course, the party were as seriously serious as serious could get, so they didn't hesitate to kill kobolds that got in their way. As for the kobolds, they didn't want to die, so they'd run away. As a result, the encirclement was too soft, and Haruhiro and the others were still able to keep fleeing.

*Scary is scary, but there's no need to be more frightened than necessary. If we overestimate the threat and panic, we'll lose the ability to do things we can actually manage.*

"It's the well…!" Haruhiro shouted. "Shihoru, you go up the ladder first! Next, Merry! The order after that will be Yume, myself, Ranta, and then Moguzo!"

First Ranta, then Merry, Yume, and Haruhiro cut open a path to the bottom of the well. This was a small well with only one rope ladder coming down. Shihoru put her hands and feet on the ladder. She got a bit muddled up, but rushing her would only have the opposite effect.

"It's fine! You don't have to rush!" As Haruhiro called up to Shihoru to say that, for an instant—he saw that shining line. There was a kobold that just happened to have its back to him. With smooth motions, Haruhiro planted his dagger into the kobold's back.

Merry started up the ladder, and Yume was trying to follow her, as well.

"Go, Haruhiro!" Ranta pulled off his thoroughly dented bucket helm, throwing it at one of the kobolds. "Take that! Exhaust! Hatred…!"

Hip-checking the kobold behind him with Exhaust, Ranta leapt forward immediately with Hatred, slashing the kobold in front of him. It was a bold and skillful move.

"Ruohhhhhhhhhhhhngh...!"

Moguzo had intimidated the nearby kobolds with War Cry. Now was the time.

Haruhiro swiftly scurried up the rope ladder. *I'm actually pretty good at this sort of thing,* he thought.

"Next! Come on, Ranta...!" he called.

"—No! Moguzo, you go next!" Ranta said, slapping Moguzo in the back with his longsword. "Hurry up! Since you're so slow...!"

"Y-yeah?!" Instead of having accepted Ranta's reasoning, it seemed more like Moguzo was surprised and just did as he was told without thinking.

Moguzo started climbing up, so Haruhiro couldn't stop now. He had to keep climbing.

"Wai—Ranta...! Hurry up...!"

"Sure!"

Haruhiro could hear his response. But there was no sign of him climbing up. Not Ranta.

Rather than Ranta, a kobold started climbing up the rope ladder.

"Damn! You!" Moguzo kicked it down, but another kobold came up after it.

"Climb up for now!" Haruhiro made it up to the fourth level and pulled Moguzo up—or tried, at least, but he was heavy. Too heavy.

"Ohhh..." Haruhiro grunted.

"We'll help!" With Merry, Yume, and Shihoru lending a hand, they somehow hauled Moguzo up onto the fourth level.

*That was great, but what about Ranta?* There was no Ranta. Instead of Ranta, kobolds came up the ladder one after another.

"Ranta...!" Haruhiro called his name, but there was no response.

*No.*

"You go on ahead...! I'll catch up later...!" In between the howling of the kobolds, they heard Ranta's voice faintly.

"What do you mean, 'later'...?! Moguzo, get that kobold that's coming up!" Haruhiro shouted.

"Hungh!" Moguzo stabbed his bastard sword at the kobold that was coming up the ladder. "Hungh, hungh, hungh...!"

With the lead kobold's face messed up good, it fell down, taking a number of other kobolds with it. The kobolds were barking noisily at the bottom, but perhaps out of fear of the same thing happening again, they didn't try to climb up.

"...The ladder!" said Shihoru, grabbing the rope ladder.

*Hey, yeah. We can just pull up the ladder.*

"Got it!" Haruhiro hurried over to Shihoru and started pulling up the ladder, but his hands stopped halfway. "...B-but."

Yume put her hands on the rim of the well, looking down. "Ranta...!"

"It's just for now...!" Shihoru said.

Haruhiro nodded, pulling up the ladder. *That's right. If the kobolds give up and go away, we can lower it again. The way things are now, Ranta can't get near the well anyway, I'm sure.*

*Ranta. Did he run away? Did he get away all right? Honestly, I have a hard time thinking he did. Ranta may have the devil's own luck, but this is just too much.*

"That ass!" Haruhiro punched the ground. "Trying to act cool, telling us to go on ahead without him...! It's not like you, man! You're supposed to be lame! What gives...?!"

No one said anything.

The kobolds were making a lot of noise down below.

*Ahh!*

*What now? What am I supposed to do now?*

Haruhiro and the rest were safe. They were bruised all over, but their wounds wouldn't keep them from walking.

Ranta was the only exception.

If Ranta were here, too, they'd leave the mines without a second thought. They'd probably head straight for the outside.

If Ranta were here.

Probably, even without Ranta, they could still make it outside.

By leaving him behind.

*Do we go save him? Go down to level five through another well and search for Ranta? Of course, it would be risky. Besides, we don't even know if Ranta's still alive. He could be dead already. If Ranta's dead, anything we do would be in vain.*

*What am I thinking? How can I think about Ranta being dead?*

*Still, the problem is, it's a genuine possibility. With that many kobolds, and with him being surrounded all by himself, it's hard to imagine he'd have gotten away.*

At the very least, Haruhiro knew he couldn't have done it. He'd likely have given up at some point.

*Then...how about Ranta?*

*He might not give up.*

"Haru," Merry called out to Haruhiro, snapping him back to his senses.

*Oh, crap.*

*I was totally lost in thought.*

"Huh? Wh-what?"

"Enemies!" she said.

"You're kidding—" is what Haruhiro wanted to think, but it was true.

When he looked in the direction Merry pointed, there were kobolds running in their direction. Elders. With workers in tow, too.

"There are a whole bunch of them!" Yume said, sounding ready to cry.

"Wh-wh-whuh..." Moguzo was confused and flustered.

Shihoru shook her head back and forth, as if trying to reject the reality of the situation, then said "W-we...we have... to run away!"

Haruhiro's mind went blank for a moment. But it was only for a moment. He didn't have time to agonize over his decision.

Haruhiro stood up. "—Let's run!"

*Grimgar of Fantasy and Ash*

## 11. That

*Man, am I awesome or what?* Ranta thought. *Actually, I'm clearly way too damn awesome. I'm a genius. Was I chosen by some god? If so, I've gotta wonder what that god was a god of. A god of darkness, like you'd expect? Was it Skullhell? Anyway, am I badass or what?*

*I mean, I'm still alive and all.*

"Man..." Ranta said with a sigh.

Even the great Ranta-sama figured he might be in trouble this time. Just maybe, he might be done for. There sure wasn't much to suggest he wasn't. Maybe this was the end. Honestly, the thought had crossed his mind.

*Nearly pissed myself back there. Didn't actually do it, though. Well, I did come pretty close.*

*Maybe I pissed myself a little—just the littlest, tiniest bit.*

Still, Ranta was alive.

*That's the important thing. The incredible thing.*

Ranta had done something no one else could've.

*I think I can boast about that. I want to praise myself silly.*

Every sentient being in this world ought to have been singing Ranta's praises.

"...Hey, you think so, too, right, Zodiac-kun?" Ranta asked, turning to the blackish purple demon floating beside his head.

Demons were minions of the dark god Skullhell that dread knights could summon with their dark magic spell, Demon Call.

Demons changed shape as the dread knight who summoned them accumulated vices, and Ranta's Zodiac-kun was shaped like the headless torso of a human with two hole-like eyes in the chest area and a slit like a mouth beneath them.

"No, no...no...no, no...not at all..." When Zodiac-kun talked, its mouth hissed and burbled as it moved. A demon's voice sounded almost like a group of children all whispering at the same time. It was pretty creepy until one got used to it.

Actually, even now that Ranta had gotten used to it, it was *still* creepy, and he got goosebumps every time he heard it.

"Still, it beats being alone..." Ranta murmured.

"Wimpy, wimpy...wimpy, wooly caterpillar...wimpy, wimpy, wimpy...caterpillar, caterpillar...caterpillar, caterpillar, caterpillar..."

"Hey, by the end, you were just repeating the word caterpillar..."

"Caterpillar, caterpillar, caterpillar... *Ehehehehehe*... Caterpillar... *Ehehehehehe*... Caterpillar, caterpillar, caterpillar..."

"That's enough out of you!" When Ranta swung his hand up to whack the demon for comedic effect, Zodiac-kun floated up to avoid him.

"*Ehehe... Ehehehehehe... Ehehehehehehe...* Caterpillar, caterpillar... *Ehehehehehehe...*"

"...Dammit. Friggin' Zodiac-kun..." Ranta hugged his knees,

pretending to sob.

Doing that just made him feel empty, so he stopped.

"Still, I'm impressed I made it up to the fourth level..." he said.

—That's right.

Ranta wasn't in the refinery on the fifth level. He was in the farm on the fourth.

Just how in the world had he cut his way out of that bloody battle? He didn't know himself how it happened, but after sending Moguzo on ahead, he'd just run around like crazy and eventually he'd ended up at another well. He did remember kicking down a number of kobolds as he'd climbed the rope ladder, though.

At least some of the kobolds from the fifth level had chased him up to the fourth, but luckily, the gate on the fence around one of the enclosures they kept those critters in had been left open.

When Ranta had raced inside it, the pigrats inside had made a frenzied rush to the entrance. That'd let him distract a good number of his pursuers. Still, while it hadn't been enough to lose all of them, it'd make him think, *I can use this.*

Ranta had gone from one pigrat or pigworm enclosure to the next, shaking off kobold pursuers little by little, and when he finally shook off the last of them—

*Here I am. Inside a pigworm enclosure.*

*There're pigworms everywhere.*

Ranta and Zodiac-kun were surrounded by pigworms.

"Still, though..." He tried poking the pigworm that was right next to him just a little bit.

*No response.*

As if it were the natural thing to do next, he tried slapping it with the palm of his hand.

*Knew it. This pigworm won't give me a response.*

"Fine, be that way!" Ranta snapped. *If that's how you want it—*

Ranta tried pinching the pigworm's thick hide. When he did, the pigworm glared at him with black eyes half-buried behind its droopy eyelids, and it let out a cry of *gufuu*.

"...D-did I make it...mad?" Ranta stammered.

"*Gufuu. Gufuu.*"

"Whoa! Hold it! Wai—Don't nuzzle up to my face, that's gross...!"

"*Bufuu. Bufufuu. Gufuu.*"

"You! Did you just lick...?! Wait, what's with your tongue?! It's too rough, it hurts!"

"*Fuu. Gufuu. Fufuu. Fuu. Fuu.*"

The pigworm rubbed up against Ranta. He tried to push it away, but it was no use. It was incredibly strong. He couldn't get away.

Finally, the pigworm wrapped its body around Ranta. If he squirmed, it'd squeeze him, but when he stayed put, the pigworm calmed down.

"...Seriously? This guy's just chilling out, isn't he? Seriously...?"

"Caterpillar, caterpillar, caterpillar... *Ehehehehehe*... Caterpillar, caterpillar... *Ehehehehehe*... Caterpillar..."

"I've got Zodiac-kun picking on me, too..." he muttered.

"Die... Die, die.... Go to Lord Skullhell's embrace... Be embraced..."

"Don't say scary stuff like that!"

"Wimpy... Wimpy, wimpy... Wimpy, wooly caterpillar... *Ehehehehehe*... Caterpillar, caterpillar, caterpillar, caterpillar, caterpillar..."

"...In the end, I'm a caterpillar, huh?"

Ranta wasn't alone. He had Zodiac-kun with him, and for some reason, this pigworm was taking to him, as well. Still, he was isolated and without support.

"This guy stinks, too..." he muttered.

It was indescribable—well, no, it was *pretty* describable, if he was blunt. The pigworm smelled of urine and feces. The environment in the pigworm pen was the worst, but if he left it, the elders on patrol might find him. Even up against an elder, he'd probably still manage it one-on-one.

*I could win. With how strong I am. Still, I'm a little tired. I don't want to push myself. If I use my true power, an elder or two'll be easy, but I kind of want to rest for a bit. Even the bold and resolute dread knight needs his rest.*

*Once I've rested good and proper, I'll move into action.*

"I've gotta get out on my own," he muttered.

*Moguzo. Yume. Shihoru. Merry.*

*And Haruhiro.*

One after another, their faces drifted across his mind.

*—This is no good.*

*They're not reliable.*

*Or rather, I can't rely on them.*

Ranta laughed derisively. "...Yeah, I know, you guys all hate my guts."

*Why? I don't remember things that happened a long time ago, so I don't know the reason.*

Anyhow, Ranta couldn't pretend to be good. Acting nice to people, being considerate, just the thought of it made him want to puke. If he didn't think something, there was nothing that could make him say it. Even when he did think something, there was a huge pile of things he still couldn't say.

*"If I act like this, they're gonna get pissed." It's not like I never think that. Sometimes I do. It's not that I don't. But, even so, I can't keep myself in check. Isn't it kind of wrong doing that? I mean, I'm me. Do I want to lie and pretend I'm a good person so that others will like me? Yeah, no. I'm not doing that.*

*I don't want to strain myself to be liked. If they don't like me, it's no skin off my back. If they want to hate me, let 'em.*

*Those who get it, get it. That's what I think. There've gotta be people out there who get it. Get what? My value? Something like that. There're probably people who can judge me fairly, and will recognize me for it, too. So, it's fine. If people don't get it, they don't have to.*

*I say that, but comrades are comrades.*

Ranta was a member of the party. He'd been contributing to the party in his own way, and he planned to keep on doing so.

*They'll understand soon enough,* he had thought. They'd realize how lucky they were that Ranta-sama was with them. Once everyone recognized how important Ranta was, their attitudes would change.

Ranta was well aware they hadn't gotten that far yet, though.

*It was too soon. I went and did that without thinking.*

—Leave this to me, you guys go on ahead...!

"Well, yeah..." Of course he had.

If they'd seen the opportunity, any man would have. He'd have to. Any man who didn't wouldn't be a man.

Even if it were a woman, yeah, a woman might do it, too. If Ranta were a woman, he'd probably do it.

So, he had no regrets. Ranta had done what he'd had to do. There'd been no other choice.

*Still, I do wish the chance could have come along later.*

Once his comrades had been forced to realize his greatness and he'd become an indispensable member of the party, if the chance had come for him to do it, the impact would've been intense.

Stupid Haruhiro would have cried like a baby. Moguzo would have wailed. As for the girls, they would've fallen for Ranta, for sure. Then, they'd have been all like, "We can't abandon our Ranta-sama! Let's go look for him, everyone! Yeah!" That's absolutely what would have happened.

*It was too soon. The time came too soon.*

"I guess it just means the times can't keep up with me, huh," Ranta muttered.

*Maybe not,* he thought, *then let out a deep sigh. I probably can't count on my comrades. Nobody'll be coming to help me. Gonna have to get out of this one on my own.*

"Die... *Ehehehehehe*... Die, caterpillar... Die... *Ehehehehehehe*... Caterpillar, caterpillar, caterpillar..."

Zodiac-kun's abuse hit him hard.

However, his master in the dread knights' guild had told him something. That a demon is like a mirror held up to its summoner. A demon is the reflection of its dread knight.

*What, this jerk is?* was what Ranta had wanted to think, but his master, Kidney Aguro, was super scary. His master wasn't here right now, but the man was so terrifying that he was still convinced he'd be killed if he doubted him.

"In other words, I've still got the power left to heap abuse on someone." Ranta smirked.

*I'm good. I've got this,* he thought. *Just you watch, Haruhiro. I'll get out of this by myself if I have to. You better be shocked later. That, and bow down to me while you're at it.*

## 12. When It's Important

When the party had made it up to the third level and finally thought they could relax a little, an elder foreman and two followers discovered them, immediately leading to a melee.

"Urkh! Oh! Uwah...!"

Haruhiro deflected Follower A's sword with his dagger, deflected it, and kept deflecting it.

His Swat skill was only good for buying time. If he got into a serious fight, this was how it went. Now he had to focus on his opponent's weapon and movement, which made it very hard to check the situation around him.

*What's going on? Is everyone okay? I'm worried. But I don't have time for worrying. Time. Buy time. Even a little of it. By doing this. Taking on one of the enemies.*

Moguzo can handle a foreman one-on-one now. Yume's never timid. She should be confidently trading blows with Follower B right now. Then we have Shihoru. Merry, too.

If Haruhiro could just stop Follower A, they ought to be able to manage this.

Though, that was only *if* he could stop it.

"Woof...!"

Follower A suddenly turned its back on him. When his eyes stopped on its swishing tail, Haruhiro thought, *Oh, no.*

Follower A spun back around, making a big swing at him with its sword. He probably couldn't deflect it, but his body acted reflexively. He'd been using Swat too much, and had developed a habit of using it whenever he was attacked.

"Whoa...!"

It went about as well as he'd expected. Haruhiro's dagger was pushed back by Follower A's sword, and when he lost his balance, Follower A pressed the attack.

"Woof! Woof! Woof! Woof...!"

"Ah! Ah! Whoa! Urkh...!" Haruhiro shouted.

He didn't have time to use Swat. Haruhiro dodged Follower A's sword, not using the minimum amount of movement possible; he couldn't show off like that. He twisted his body as hard as he could, throwing himself out of the way.

He wouldn't last like this. He knew that. He wanted to keep his cool, but he just couldn't. He always ended up panicking despite himself.

"—Ack...!" he shouted.

*It cut me. On my left arm. Just a bit above the elbow.*

*It's shallow. I'm fine,* he told himself quickly. *Wait, no, it's bleeding. Pretty badly, too. It hurts. What the hell? Oh, come on, please. Who am I saying "please" to? I don't really know. If I had to guess, Follower A? I'm saying "don't pick on me like this," maybe? Of course, even if I asked it to, it's not going to listen.*

"Woof...!" Follower A turned its back to him again.

*It's the same trick as before. I just have to dodge when it comes,* thought Haruhiro. *It's so obvious. When I know what it's doing, that technique isn't scary at all.*

Haruhiro did exactly that. He dodged.

*Jump back. Good, Follower A's attack won't reach me here—*

Or it shouldn't have, but Follower A suddenly did a somersault and leapt at him, which astonished Haruhiro.

"Wha—"

*That wasn't its sword. It kicked me. Right in the chest.*

Haruhiro was sent flying and landed flat on his butt.

Follower A came after him, trying to get in an attack while he was down.

*Oh, crap. He's gonna get me.*

"Blame...!"

*A light.*

*It's Merry's magic.*

The blinding light struck Follower A. It reeled backwards, staggering.

While Haruhiro was getting back to his feet, Merry closed in on Follower A.

"Smash...!"

With a big swing of her priest's staff, she landed a punishing blow on the side of Follower A's face.

It was a combo chaining Blame with Smash.

*Magnificent,* Haruhiro thought, awed. —Wait, now's not the time to be impressed...!

Follower A was unsteady on its feet. Haruhiro slipped around behind Follower A, grappling it and jamming his dagger in under its jaw.

*Spider.*

Immediately backing away, for an instant, his eyes met Merry's. "Nice save!" he said, looking around the area.

*Moguzo's got the upper hand with the foreman. Yume's struggling against Follower B. Looks like she's been hurt. Better lend her a hand.*

After that, Shihoru used the Shadow Bond spell to stall the foreman, Moguzo took it out with a completely one-sided onslaught, and after that, they just had to gang up on Follower B and finish it. Haruhiro and the others quickly collected just the talismans from the kobold corpses and had Merry heal their wounds, able to breathe the sigh of relief they'd been denied until now.

"Even without Ranta, we managed to work things out, huh," Yume said, smiling a little. However, it was a smile tinged with exhaustion. Besides, like Haruhiro, Yume had been wounded in the last battle, too. It might've been more accurate to say that it wasn't so much that they'd managed to work things out as that somehow things had managed to work out.

"...Still, that was a close call...I think," Shihoru said, hanging her head. "I really think that Yume and Haruhiro-kun aren't meant to be on the front line... Ah, I don't mean to put either of you down by that..."

"I know," Haruhiro smiled to Shihoru. It was a forced smile, though. "It's just like you're saying. Yume and I aren't the type that can take on an enemy and just do our best. Well...especially me. I dunno how to put it, but, you know—when things go bad, the enemy ends up making me run around, and even when they go well, I end up making the enemy run around while I try to hang in there. When that happens, I'm sure it must be a little hard for Merry and Shihoru. The battlefield turns into a mess. I think it gets hard to keep a handle on the situation, ya know."

"Ranta moves around a lot, too, though," Merry said.

She might've been trying to cover for him, but Haruhiro had to shake his head. "Yeah, sure. But in Ranta's case, he's trying to lure enemies in to fight him one-on-one. If I try to get involved, he gets pissed. He's a moron, but if we leave him to it, he always keeps one of them busy. I think that's a big deal. Also, he..."

*I don't want to acknowledge it. It's just not fair. It's the truth, though, so I will.*

Haruhiro sighed. "—He's definitely getting stronger. Faster than anyone else. I dunno if it's because of the way he uses his skills like crazy, but he's able to fire them off one after another really fast. He's become a real asset in battle. There's no doubt about it."

*Maybe more of one than useless me. He* came close to saying that, but Haruhiro managed to stop himself. *No need to be self-deprecating. No good can come from it.*

"W-we should go save..." Moguzo started to say, but stopped short.

"Now, listen." Yume looked at Haruhiro with upturned eyes. One of her cheeks was puffed up. "Listen, about Yume, you probably all know this already, but she hates Ranta. When Ranta calls her boobs tiny, Yume, she feels really hurt. Even when she asks him to stop, Ranta won't stop. When a person's actin' like that, it's hard to like them, even if someone asks you to."

"Yeah," Haruhiro nodded, telling her to go on.

"So, you know..." Yume looked down, puffing up both of her cheeks this time. "So, Yume still hates Ranta, but just havin' him gone, we're already havin' a pretty hard time of it. But for Ranta, it's Haru-kun, Moguzo, Shihoru and Merry-chan and Yume, that's five people. Just think how hard it'd be for any of us if the other five went missin' all at once..."

"Yume..." Shihoru put an arm around Yume's shoulder.

"When Yume thinks about it..." Yume was tearing up. "If it were Yume, and she were in a place like this, and five people, eeeeveryone, just went missin', she'd feel real lonely, wouldn't she? Yume's sure she wouldn't be able to take a single step after that. When she wonders what Ranta's doin'..."

"First of all..." Haruhiro began to say, then closed his mouth tight, breathing through his nose.

*Having to think about things seriously like this is pretty rough, I think. Even if it feels like it's driving me crazy, I need to come to a calm decision somehow.*

*Can I do that? Is that something I'm capable of? Honestly, I won't know until I try. Even once I do try, I still may not know. Whether I really am calm or not. How am I to judge? Who do I ask? "Hey, do I seem calm now?" Am I supposed to just ask like that?*

*Yeah, I can't do that.*

Everyone focused their attention on Haruhiro, waiting for his next words.

They were relying on Haruhiro.

*I'll just have to do it.*

"I can't say for sure whether Ranta is safe or not. However, I want to act on the assumption that he is. If we don't do that, whatever actions we take will lose all meaning. So, Ranta's still alive. If he's alive, I want to save him."

Considering the situation, Haruhiro couldn't push the job off onto anyone else. He couldn't throw his hands up and run away from the whole thing, either.

"First, we go down to the fourth level," he said. "If we can make it, we'll go down as far as the fifth. However, we don't take any risks. Ranta stayed down there so we could get away. Setting aside whether he should've or not, if we get ourselves wiped out for his sake, the risk he took will have been in vain."

*I'm terrible,* thought Haruhiro. *I can't say this out loud, but if this had been any one of our comrades other than Ranta, I might have struggled longer before I found an answer.*

*Ranta.*

*It's probably because it's you that I'm able to stay somewhat calm.*

"Definitely don't do anything reckless," he added. "We'll prioritize our own safety, and if it gets bad, we turn back. For now, we'll go outside. We'll think about what we'll do after that once we get there. Any objections?"

He didn't think for a moment that anyone would raise their hand.

Indeed, nobody did.

Haruhiro had made the decision, and everyone else had just agreed with it. Haruhiro worried that the incredible weight of responsibility, of uncertainty, or of terror, would paralyze him.

But that wasn't how it was. Actually, if anything, he felt relieved. The decision had already been made. Now, he'd have no choice but to get serious about doing it. He might even be in the right mindset already.

"Okay, let's go," he said. "Ranta's waiting for us."

## 13. Duo

*I can't just stay in this pigworm pen forever. These guys are getting too friendly, and it's kind of gross.*

"Still, I'll miss you," Ranta said his farewell to the pigworm that was rubbing up to him. "...Yeah, no, I won't miss you at all. Don't you dare try to follow me. If you do, I'm frying you whole and then eating you, you got that?"

His words fell on deaf ears, however, as the pigworm continued to oink and nuzzle up to him.

"Stupid, clingy pigworm. This is goodbye!" Ranta shook off the pigworm as it chased him, and leapt over the fence. The only trusty follower he needed was his demon, Zodiac-kun.

"Wimpy, wooly caterpillar... *Ehehehehe*... Caterpillar, caterpillar... *Keehehehehe*... Caterpillar, caterpillar, caterpillar, caterpillar..."

"...You shut up for a bit."

"No, *you* shut up... *Keehehehehehe*... Forever..."

"What, are you telling me to die?!"

"*Ehehehehehehehe*..."

"Get lost, Zodiac-kun…"

No, instead of doing that, Zodiac-kun brought its gash-like mouth close to Ranta's ear.

"It's here…here… *Ehehehehe*… One of the ones trying to kill you…"

"What?!" Panicked, Ranta looked around.

There it was. An elder. The type that carried a metal whip and steel wire. Fortunately, it wasn't looking his way, but it was coming closer.

After hesitating a moment, Ranta jumped into a different pigworm pen from the one he'd been in before. If he dove in with the pigworms, the elder wouldn't spot him at first glance.

There were pigrat pens in the vicinity as well, but after having seen them greedily devour a kobold cadaver, Ranta decided he'd rather not go in there. *I wouldn't want to get eaten, after all.*

And so, after frolicking with the pigworms—no, no, not frolicking with them, they were just nuzzling up to him, all right?—One, no, two of them became attached to him this time, licking his face relentlessly. The pigworms' tongues were rough, so it hurt. It hurt so bad that he was worried they'd draw blood.

*Oh, crap.*

"…Damn, I'm popular."

"Popular… Popular… *Keehehehehe*… Popular… *Ehehehehe*… Popular…"

"Zodiac-kun, you…"

*One of these days, I'm gonna give you such a pounding,* Ranta silently vowed to himself.

Today, however, was not that day.

Zodiac-kun was being felt up by the pigworms just like Ranta, but the demon could do no more than just stay by its dread knight's side.

As he accumulated more vices, his demon gained access to special abilities.

From 0 to 10 vices, at rank 1, it'd warn when enemies were approaching.

If it felt like it.

From 11 to 40 vices, once it'd reached rank 2, it'd also whisper in the enemies' ears to disrupt them.

When it felt like it.

Once Ranta got over 41 vices and his demon reached rank 3, it'd do things like trip enemies to disrupt them.

Of course, this was also only if it felt like it.

Also, this was when the sun went down and the dark god Skullhell's natural enemy the god of light Lumiaris' powers were weakened. At rank 1, he couldn't even summon his demon during the day. From rank 2 onwards, the demon acted as if he was one rank lower during daylight hours.

Ranta was currently rank 3.

He couldn't be totally sure since he was underground, but it probably wasn't evening yet. Even so, Zodiac-kun would still use its rank 2 abilities for Ranta.

...When it felt like it.

"As I accumulate vice, my demon powers up, and it'll do what I want more often," Ranta said. "That's what my master said, at least..."

"Really? Is that really true? *Keehehehehe...* Did he *really* say that? *Ehehehehehe...*"

"He said it, okay?"

"You're being tricked... Tricked... *Ehehehehe...* You're being tricked... *Keehehehehehehe...*"

"Don't say ominous things like that."

"Ominous... Ominous... Ominous... *Keehehehe*... Today, you'll die... *Ehehehe*..."

"...Dammit. *This* is why I don't like summoning you, Zodiac-kun..."

*Still, Zodiac-kun does help out sometimes, like how it warned me about the enemy approaching just now. Besides—if I were alone, I'd be feeling a little lonely right now.*

*No,* Ranta shook his head.

"...I'm not lonely. As if I'd ever be lonely. I mean, the word 'lonely' isn't even in my dictionary."

"You're putting on a brave front... *Ehehehehe*... It's a thin front, thin front... *Keehe*... *Keehehe*... A skin and bones front..."

"I'm not putting on a brave front, and what's a skin and bones front supposed to be?"

Well, anyway, getting pissed at every little thing it says isn't going to help, but thanks to Zodiac-kun, I'm not bored at least. *Ranta nodded to himself.*

"That's an important factor, you know. Yeah, a factor. Damn, that word's cool. Not an element, a factor. Though maybe it just sounds cool 'cause I'm the one saying it? In other words, that'd mean I'm cool, huh? Well, that was already obvious. Whew... Hey, Zodiac-kun? Not going to poke fun at me?"

"..."

"Why do you have to go all quiet at times like this? Say something."

"......"

"Hey, Zodiac-kun."

"........."

"Hey, I'm talking to you. Hey? Zodiac-kun?"

"............"

"Wait, huh? What? Is something up? Zodiac-kun? Are you all right?!"

"..............."

"Z-Zodiac-kun?!"

"Ha... Tricked you... *Keehehehe*... You got tricked..."

"You jerk...!"

Ranta tried punching Zodiac-kun, but his fist bounced off the demon, and there was no sign his Iron Fist of Retribution had had any effect whatsoever.

"You're supposed to be a dread knight... You don't even know how to inflict damage on a demon...? *Keehehehe*..." Zodiac-kun taunted.

"Y-you idiot, it's not like that. Come on, you're *my* demon. What would I want to hurt you for?"

"You... *Keehe*... When you say that...are you serious...?"

"Damn straight, I am! You think I could say it if I wasn't?"

"...Go die a million times."

"Why?!"

"*Keehehehe... Keehe... Keehehehehehehe... Keehehe... Keehehehehehehehehehe...*"

*This is pointless. Acting out something like a husband and wife comedy routine with Zodiac-kun's not going to help my situation. It's been fun, but I don't have time for this.*

"Sitting still's just not my style. Besides, hiding won't do me any good," Ranta said.

Even if he stayed here, he didn't think help would be coming.

*It isn't coming...right? They wouldn't come...would they? Yeah, no. There's no way they'd come.*

*—What am I getting my hopes up for? It's pathetic. I'm a man, dammit!*

"If I get found, whatever happens, happens." Ranta told himself, deciding it was time to make a gamble. This was more his style, he thought, satisfied.

Pushing the pigworms away from him, he jumped out of the pen.

*I've still got a long way to go... I hope,* he thought, so he didn't sprint. He ran straight down the path between the pens.

"Easy. This is a cinch."

There were a lot of workers in the darkshroom, holly-fern, and lightflower fields, and they had a clear, unobstructed view across them, so it was dangerous there. However, in this area where the pigrat and pigworm pens were concentrated, an elder or worker only came around on patrol once in a while, so it wasn't so bad by comparison.

The fences around the pens were pretty high, too, so if he kept himself low to the ground, he wouldn't stand out.

*Was I being too cautious before?* Ranta wondered.

"I'm so giddy I could skip, heh heh!" Ranta grinned.

After Ranta got carried away and started skipping, a worker stepped out from between two pens on his left and they collided.

"Whoa!" "Yelp!"

It surprised him, but he didn't have time to be surprised right now. Ranta threw himself at the worker and grappled with it. He did that because he didn't think he could afford the time to draw his longsword, but what was he going to do now...? He had a flash of inspiration.

These days, Haruhiro used a skill called Spider sometimes. That was it. He didn't know how to do it, but he figured he could just imitate what he'd seen and figure out the rest on his own.

"D-don't move!" First, Ranta put the worker in a full nelson.

Of course, the worker thrashed around and resisted. It was incredibly strong, but Ranta was desperate, too. He locked down both the enemy's arms with his own. When he tried to wrap his legs around the front of his opponent's legs, though, it didn't quite go as planned and he ended up tumbling over along with the worker.

"—Urkh!"

As he was rolling around with the worker, he struck his head a number of times. With it elbowing him in the side, too, he was in a lot of pain.

*The technique looked simple enough, but it's harder to do than I thought. For now, it doesn't feel like keeping the worker's arms bound like this is getting me anywhere.*

"Gotta get its throat...!" Letting its arms free, Ranta went to wring the worker's neck. He wrapped both arms around it and squeezed hard.

When it found it couldn't breathe, the worker flailed about even more frantically than before, trying to throw Ranta off.

*I won't let you throw me off,* Ranta thought.

"Arrrgh...!" he shouted.

The worker scratched him in the face. It jabbed its fingers into his mouth, tearing the corner of his lips open. Ranta bit the worker's fingers and kept on squeezing its neck.

"Hunnnnnnnngahhhhhh...!"

Finally, *finally,* the worker went limp.

"...Did I kill it? No!" Unable to believe it was over, Ranta didn't let go of the worker's neck for another five to ten seconds.

*Is it safe now?*

He checked to see if it was breathing. It was not. It looked like it was dead.

Ranta pushed the worker's corpse away from him. He tried to get up, but he didn't have the strength.

Zodiac-kun floated nearby, looking down at Ranta. "*Keehehe...* What are you doing...? You're inexperienced... Unripe... An unripe grape... *Ehe...*"

"...How am I a grape?"

*Still, that was a close call, huh?*

*Nah, it wasn't a close call at all, was it? I was absolutely, totally fine, wasn't I?*

"Yeah, that's my story and I'm sticking to it."

With some effort, Ranta got up. *Now, what to do with the body?* First, he took the talisman from it. That put him in a better mood, and he almost wanted to shout in celebration as he chucked the worker's remains into the pigrat pen.

"And that's that...whoa...?!"

*There was a lot of barking.*

*It's a kobold. No, kobolds. There're a bunch of them coming my way from that direction.*

"Fight...dread knight... *Keehehehehehe...* Fight them... *Keehehehehehehe...*"

"No, I'm not gonna fight! There's too many for me to handle, obviously!"

"Wimpy, wooly caterpillar... Caterpillar, caterpillar, caterpillar... *Ehehehehehe...*"

"Dammit, Zodiac-kun...!"

Ranta turned heel and ran.

*My body feels heavy. On top of that, my whole face—especially my torn lip—hurts. How bad is the tear? This is awful. What'll I do if I've been turned into a slit-mouthed man? My handsome face would be ruined. Guess that's not what I should be worrying about though, huh?*

When he turned around, it looked like the kobolds had almost caught up to him.

He wanted to whine and complain, but he knew Zodiac-kun would just mock him for it. He wasn't sure he could survive Zodiac-kun's barbed tongue in his current mental state. So Ranta decided to keep quiet, not look back, and run as hard as he could.

*Grimgar of Fantasy and Ash*

## 14. A Boy

"...Isn't it kind of noisy over that way?" Haruhiro asked, pointing.

Everyone turned to look in that direction.

"Hmm?" Yume brought her hands up to her eyes like a pair of binoculars. "...Hmm. It's hard to see with all the fences, but somethin' that looks like a head is bobbin' up and down over there."

"I hear kobolds barking, too." Merry was listening closely. "There seem to be a large number of kobolds over there."

"Do you think...?" Shihoru said, clutching her staff.

Moguzo nodded. "I-it could be Ranta-kun...maybe?"

Haruhiro and the others were on the fourth level, the farm. They'd come down from the third level to the fourth and they had just a little further to go before they would reach a well down to the fifth level when Haruhiro noticed something strange.

"Did he make it up from the fifth level to the fourth on his own...?" Haruhiro wondered.

*I always knew he was a stubborn guy,* he thought. *It may not be the most incredible feat ever, but it's still pretty impressive if he pulled that off.*

At the very least, Ranta had a greater ability to survive than your average person. That never-say-die attitude was something none of the others had.

"Let's go!" Haruhiro said.

They all looked at one another and then headed towards the uproar. They went quickly, but carefully. If they ended up being chased around, too, it'd defeat the purpose.

*Still, isn't it kind of impossible to approach a place where a large number of kobolds are running around without being discovered...?* Haruhiro had everyone else stay back, poking his head out from behind one of the pens.

"...Oh."

There they were. A whole bunch of them. The kobolds were running this way and that, sometimes jumping over the fences into or out of the pens, barking madly like dogs all the while.

Haruhiro watched them for a while. The kobolds didn't even look in his direction. Not that he minded.

Haruhiro pulled his head back in. "...Not happening."

That was the only possible conclusion.

If they went any further, the kobolds would be sure to find them. If they were willing to be found, they could try to lure the kobolds away to help Ranta, who was probably on the run or hiding, but even if they did that, they couldn't be sure they'd be able to draw all the kobolds to them.

Besides, compared to the five of them, Haruhiro thought Ranta might have an easier time running around and hiding.

If Haruhiro and the rest of the group found themselves pursued by kobolds again, there was no guarantee they'd all be able to get away.

In fact, it was best to assume they wouldn't. They needed to throw away any optimistic notions like that.

He really didn't want the kobolds to find them. How they could help Ranta without being found, however, was something he was having a hard time coming up with. It was a matter of priorities.

What should the order of priorities be here?

*Right now, what's most important? And what comes next after that?*

The most important priority was...

...keeping the five of them safe.

Saving Ranta came after that.

That order couldn't be changed. It had to be this way.

Even if it weren't Ranta who needed saving—if it had been Yume or Shihoru, or even Moguzo or Merry—Haruhiro would have had to make the same decision. He believed that was his role as leader.

"We're getting out of here," Haruhiro said, shaking his head. "I don't doubt that Ranta's in this area, but if we get found by the kobolds, too, and make this into an even bigger uproar than it already is, the situation will only get worse. Kobolds don't exactly seem all that patient. They give up pretty quickly. I'm sure they have work that needs doing, too. So...things'll settle down eventually. Let's look for Ranta once that happens."

"But, what if..." Shihoru said hesitantly. "What if Ranta gets caught before that and... Oh, I'm sorry, I just..."

"If he does..." Yume bit her lip and grimaced. "...If that happens, we won't be seein' Ranta alive again, to say the least."

"You're right," said Merry, her face a bit pale.

Moguzo let out a long, deep sigh.

"The one who made the decision..." Haruhiro clutched his thighs tightly. "...was me. No matter what happens, the responsibility is mine alone."

"No, that's not right," Yume shook her head vigorously. "It's not just *your* responsibility, Haru-kun. This is somethin' we all have to—"

"No, it is."

He was glad his voice didn't tremble there. He didn't want to show off his pathetic weakness any more than he had to. It didn't matter so much when there was nothing important happening, but not right now. Now was not the time for it.

"If everyone does what I decide, the responsibility is mine," Haruhiro explained. "I don't know, I can't really explain it well, but that's how it has to be. I can't handle this without all of you supporting me, but still. I think if we're just supporting one another, we'll still be weak. A core...a central pillar... I think the party needs someone like that. The problem is, I'm not sure I can do it... Well, I plan to try at least. I'll do my best. So, I want you to let me carry that burden."

Yume suddenly slapped Haruhiro on the back. "Haru-kun, now you're actin' like a boy."

"...I-I'm a guy, you know? Always have been."

"No, Yume didn't mean it like that. Umm, let's see... Uhh, Yume doesn't really know what she meant, but she sure thought you were actin' like a boy there. Yume's gonna follow you, Haru-kun."

"Huh? Uh, sure. Thanks. Weird as that sounds to say..."

When Yume'd said she'd follow him, it'd made Haruhiro's heart skip a beat. When a girl said something like that, it was hard for him not to read more into it. It wasn't good for his heart.

Of course, it probably just meant that Yume was accepting him as the leader for now.

"Um..." Shihoru lowered her head for some reason. "Haruhiro, let me say thanks in advance, for everything..."

"Th-thanks. ...But why?"

"...It just seemed like the thing to say," she murmured.

"Okay..."

Moguzo grunted and gave him a thumbs-up.

Unsure what to do for a moment, Haruhiro returned the thumbs-up. Next, Merry extended a hand to him. After hurriedly wiping the palm of his own hand on his cloak, Haruhiro took Merry's hand.

*Her skin's ridiculously smooth,* he thought. *Merry's hand. It's so smooth.*

Haruhiro checked the area where they thought Ranta was once more.

*Yeah, nothing's changed. Charging in there would be suicide.*

"Let's pull back far enough that we can just tell what's going on," Haruhiro said to the others, adding, "Ranta's fine. If this could kill him, he'd be dead many times over by now."

Of course, that was just to assuage their worries. His comrades must have known it, too. Even so, they all nodded. He was grateful for that.

*—I don't need you coming back to haunt me. That'd be the absolute worst.* As they left the area, Haruhiro whispered in his mind, *So don't die, Ranta.*

*Grimgar of Fantasy and Ash*

## 15. The Fall and Rise of the Dread Knight

"...Ow, that hurts..."

Ranta pressed down on his left arm with his right hand, still holding his longsword with his right arm. He tried gripping his left hand, but it made him groan in pain when he did.

That was no good. He couldn't groan right now.

Ranta was in hiding.

Like always, he was hiding in the middle of a pigworm pen—or in the middle of the pigworms, to be more precise.

He was being sheltered by the great and respectable pigworms, to be even more precise.

Ranta was hiding in a group of pigworms that had gathered in the corner of one pen. Alone.

Now, he was truly alone.

The demon Zodiac-kun had taken its leave. The spell he used to summon his demon, Demon Call, had a time limit on it. Thirty minutes after being called, the demon would return to the dark god Skullhell's side. Ranta didn't have the willpower to summon Zodiac-kun again now that the demon was gone. *If I did, I'd just receive a torrent of abuse that'd depress me more...*

With a million—or at least it felt that way—kobolds chasing after him, even the great Ranta-sama who had run around with such magnificence and skill was exhausted now.

He was injured, too. He'd taken so many wounds.

In particular, the wound on his left arm was so deep that he couldn't move it properly. The pain from his left arm was so bad that he couldn't even tell where else he was injured. It was so serious that he didn't even want to check what the wound looked like and how much he was bleeding.

His entire left arm felt like it was pounding. With each throb, he could feel the blood flowing out of it.

"Hahh... Hahh... Hahh..." Ranta suddenly noticed he was panting and gasping.

"I-I'm gonna cry...★" He tried saying as cutely as he could, but it didn't make him feel the least bit better.

*A naked dance. I wanna see a naked dance. I want some super hot chick to dance naked in front of me. No, naked's not good enough. I want her wearing something, at least. Maybe just her underwear.*

*Merry. —Hmm. Not quite. Merry's too beautiful. My imagination can't handle that. Guess it's gotta be Shihoru. She's busty, after all. That's nice. I like 'em big. Yume's not bad either, mind you. Big tits are nice and all, but there're other things that are important, too. Like her face. Yume's more my type there. Yeah.*

*...Yeah, it's no good.*

*It feels too realistic. Besides, we're comrades. We're always together. Or we were, at least. When I think of her like that, it's kind of awkward.*

*Well, whatever. Guess it doesn't matter anymore.*

*They're not coming. Well, that's a given. Of course, they wouldn't be. There's no way they'd come. I'm not expecting anything, okay?*

Ranta was going to have to get out of the mines by himself.

Could he do it?

Until a little while ago, he'd fully intended to do so. He'd been convinced he could. Or at the very least, he'd tried to convince himself he could.

Now, he thought it might be too difficult.

It hurt.

It hurt, it hurt, it hurt.

He couldn't use his left arm at all with it like this. If he ran around and moved his body vigorously, it'd affect the wound. He'd end up moaning in pain. He couldn't bear any more of that throbbing pain which made his brain shudder.

*—I can't go on. I can't make it any further. Now way, no how.*

*"Like hell I can't!" ...is what I'd like to shout and blow away my weakness. If I could do it, I would.*

*Why did things turn out like this?*

*Because I tried to act cool, huh. Telling Moguzo to go on ahead. I never should've done that. I wish I hadn't. Why'd I even do it? Because I wanted to try saying it once? I wanted to say that cool line that I've always admired? Was that seriously all there was to it?*

*No, that's not it, right?*

*—I wanted their recognition.*

*If I did something self-sacrificing like that, I hoped they'd all think, "Ranta's so awesome." I think that was part of it.*

*I am me, others are others, and no matter what other people think of me, I'm totally fine—When I said that, it was a lie. If possible, I want people to think well of me. I want to be liked. To be seen as valuable. It's not that I don't know what I ought to do. That's what I have to do, right? Act like I think a good person would. Think about everyone. Be considerate. If you do that, all you need is a handsome face and you're set.*

*Ha. That's Manato. I can't be him. I'm not Manato. I can't ever be like Manato. It's too late, anyway. Way too late. Nobody thinks well of me. Nobody likes me. Nobody values me.*

*Though, I was pretty good there. With the "Moguzo, you go on ahead" bit. If they managed to get out, maybe they'll think "Thank you, Ranta, it's all because of you." Ahh. Man, for that moment, I was so cool.*

*That's enough, I guess.*

After doing something good in the end—Having saved his comrades, Ranta dies in the Cyrene Mines.

"...Will you all remember me...once in a while?" he mumbled.

The pigworms started oinking and vigorously licking his face.

"No, wait, guys, I didn't mean you! You're not the ones I meant!"

He had been feeling all sentimental, and now the pigworms had ruined it all. Well, maybe that was for the best.

If he was going to die, being crushed by pigworms wasn't how he wanted to go out. He wanted a better death than that. He should fight hard and fall gloriously.

"...Yeah."

Ranta pushed the pigworms off him and climbed over the fence.

Not long ago— how long, he honestly didn't know—the place had been overrun with kobolds, but now it was desolate.

"Did they give up already...?"

*Spineless mutts.* Ranta grinned. *—If it's like this, maybe I can make*

*it out of here?*

He gave his longsword a test swing with his right hand. It made his left arm hurt a little, but it was nothing he didn't think he could grit his teeth and bear.

"Well, I'd never die so easily, would I? Now that I think about it."

As he walked along, humming to himself, suddenly a doubt crossed his mind. —*Did those guys really abandon me?*

*They're a bunch of losers, but they're not bad folks, really. I'm sure they hate me and all, but I'm a comrade. Maybe they wouldn't abandon me so quickly? Actually, even if they wanted to, maybe they'd feel it was too harsh and not be able to go through with it...?*

Just maybe, Ranta's comrades might be searching for him. There was a non-zero chance of it.

"Don't do that..." Ranta sighed.

*You're a bunch of losers, okay? Going and risking yourselves for my sake just doesn't suit you. That's something that a guy like, say, me would be doing.*

If his comrades were searching for him, and any of them were to lose their lives because of it...

"That's not funny," he said abruptly. A cold chill ran down his spine, and Ranta shuddered.

*No. No matter what, I don't want that. I don't want to incur a huge debt like that. Stop it, please.*

If his voice could reach his distant comrades, he wanted to tell them he was fine, and to get themselves out of the mines right away.

He wouldn't go so far as to say they should return to Alterna. If possible, he hoped they'd wait outside for him.

"...Whoa." Ranta leaned against the fence. For a moment, his left arm throbbed, but this was nothing to him.

A kobold worker had come out from around a corner a little ways ahead. It hadn't noticed him yet, but it was only a matter of time. He'd have to kill it.

The decision made, Ranta acted swiftly. He didn't run, because that'd affect his wound. He closed in on the worker with smoothly sliding steps. He got up to within two meters of it.

The worker turned to face him. In that moment, Ranta stepped in to close the gap.

"…!"

Anger.

No.

This wasn't just Anger.

This was Anger 2.0: Silent Anger.

Ranta's longsword brilliantly pierced the worker's throat. The worker was flailing around, but with its throat taken out, it couldn't make a sound.

Ranta gave his longsword a twist, kicking the worker away from him. He stomped on its head, grinding his boot in. The worker stopped moving in no time. Ranta crouched down.

—*It hurts. My left arm. It hurrrrrts…*

However, as he stayed still and tried to bear it, the pain lessened.

Ranta tore the talisman from the worker's corpse, nodding to himself in approval.

"I'm gonna do this! One mutt at a time."

*Grimgar of Fantasy and Ash*

## 16. Wish and Determination

There had been a visible—er, no, an audible—change now.

It had gotten quiet.

Haruhiro and the others were hiding out in an empty pen, one without pigrats or pigworms. It was some distance from where they thought Ranta was, but there'd been a great clamor from that area until just recently.

Now, something had changed. There was almost no sound at all.

What did that indicate?

Had Ranta been caught, or had he escaped?

If he had gotten away, he might well have gone up to the third level. That thought suddenly occurred to Haruhiro, worrying him because he'd never even considered the possibility before.

*If I were smarter, all the possible outcomes would come to mind, and I'd be able to quickly choose the one with the greatest chance of success. Or would I?* Sadly, Haruhiro couldn't imagine himself ever being that intelligent. He'd just have to make do with what he had.

"Let's move. We'll go look for Ranta. We'll find him..." *I think, probably,* Haruhiro almost said, but he fell silent.

"It's okay," Merry said, clapping him on the shoulder. "Haru, you should handle things in the way that suits you best."

"Yeah, yeah," Yume agreed, and then, for reasons he didn't quite understand, patted Haruhiro on the head. "Haru-kun, you're Haru-kun because being Haru-kun makes you Haru-kun."

*I don't get what you're trying to say, or rather it seems so straightforward that it has no meaning whatsoever, but being patted on the head felt nice, if embarrassing, so, oh well, I guess it's fine.*

Moguzo stood up, punctuating it with a grunt as if to psych himself up.

Shihoru was taking deep breaths to calm herself.

The party moved into action.

First, they headed to the area where they thought Ranta maybe, potentially, was.

*Like I thought, there aren't many kobolds,* Haruhiro thought. *Or actually, there are none. It's quiet.*

*Too quiet.*

As they walked through a gap between the pigrat and pigworm pens, Haruhiro suddenly got a bad feeling.

*No matter what's happened, it's just not right for it to be so quiet. Has Ranta been caught by the kobolds?*

Haruhiro had a strong urge to shout out Ranta's name.

*Not that I'm gonna do it. It'd be weird. Though I guess that's not the problem, huh. It'd be a bad idea to raise my voice now.*

From their expressions, each of his comrades seemed to have their own thought about this. They probably weren't imagining a happy outcome.

"We don't know yet," Haruhiro said in a whisper, then reflected that his wording could have been a bit stronger.

*If I were going to say anything, I ought to have said I was sure he was alive. It's always half-measures with me. I'm glad my comrades encourage me to be myself, but I need to work on fixing my bad points. Am I even capable of that? Are people able to change so easily?*

*Awooooooooooooooooooooooooooooooooooooooooooooo...*

"Just now—" Merry said, stopping in her tracks.

Yume looked around the area. "...Did they find us?"

"No," Shihoru opened her eyes wide, shaking her head a little.

Moguzo drew his bastard sword and got into a fighting stance. "Ranta-kun."

*Where? To our left? I only heard the distinctive sound of kobolds howling once, but it came from that direction. Still, there weren't that many of them—or I didn't feel like there were. At the very least, it hasn't turned into a major disturbance yet.*

*What do I do?*

Haruhiro started running. "Let's go!"

*Is this okay? I may be putting everyone in danger. Am I sure I'm not making a mistake?*

*If it looks dangerous, we'll just turn back. Yeah. We're not in a critical situation just yet.*

*It frustrates me that I keep making excuses like this and dragging my feet. I want to be a decisive leader. Can I become one? If I can't, I can't, but I'd be fine with just looking like one. I want to pretend to be decisive. You know, that's cooler in some ways. I'm sure it'd reassure everyone, too.*

*There.*

*I see kobolds running.*

*There're three, maybe four. No, five. There're five. One elder, and the rest look like workers. Not numbers we need to worry about.*

The kobolds were chasing someone. Or rather, they already had someone surrounded. There was a single, armed human surrounded by kobolds.

That guy had a longsword in his right hand and was swinging it around. He was trying to shake off the kobolds pursuing him, but it wasn't going well at all.

He leapt straight back, putting distance between him and the kobolds. Or tried at least, but they soon caught up to him.

"Ranta...!" Haruhiro shouted.

Hearing that, Ranta looked like he'd seen a ghost.

*No, man, that ought to be my line,* thought Haruhiro, but when he thought about it, Ranta hadn't said anything. *Not my line—my what, then? Guess it doesn't matter. I don't have time to think about it.*

While Ranta was standing still after having stopped out of surprise, one of the workers sprung on him and pushed him down.

"Whoa...?!" Ranta cried.

"We're coming to save you now!" Haruhiro shouted.

*One of them's got Ranta pinned. The other four are also targeting Ranta, and they're not paying attention to us. We can pull this off.*

"Everyone attack! All at once!" By the time he said that, Haruhiro could already see that hazy line of light. The line snaked from Haruhiro's dagger to a worker, then to the elder's back.

*That's one long line,* thought Haruhiro.

Even without actively thinking about it, his body moved as if being controlled by someone else.

First, a quick thrust for the worker. Next, he stabbed his dagger into the elder. He didn't know quite how to describe the response he felt when he struck a vital point. It was like a tightening in his chest.

*Yeah, I got it,* he realized when it happened.

While Haruhiro was making short work of a worker and the elder, Moguzo was using his specialty, the Thanks Slash, to cut a worker down. Merry used her priest's staff to strike another worker, and then Shihoru hit it with Shadow Beat. Once Yume used a chain combo of Brush Clearer and Diagonal Cross to chase it into a corner, Moguzo used Thanks Slash.

"God! Dammit!" Ranta was still being held down by a worker.

Haruhiro silently ran over to that worker, grappled it from behind, then slipped his dagger under its chin as he pulled it down. Spider.

"Healing!" Merry helped Ranta to sit up and immediately started healing him with light magic.

Ranta's shoulders were heaving with heavy breaths. He glared sideways at Haruhiro. "...Don't just call a guy's name out of nowhere. I nearly died of shock, you dolt."

*Still, he's in a terrible state,* Haruhiro thought. *Merry started by healing that one wound on his left arm that looked pretty deep, but his face is a real mess, too, so it's hard to get too mad at him.*

"Sorry," Haruhiro apologized earnestly.

Ranta turned and looked away.

"Ohhh?" Yume circled around in front of the direction Ranta was now facing, then opened her eyes wide. "Ranta, are you cryin'?"

"I am not!"

"But your eyes're all watery."

"Yeah, because I hurt all over!"

"There's no need to get all mad. We're lucky, bein' able to see each other alive again like this, you know."

"I wanted to see you guys!" Ranta said, then hurriedly followed "—N-no! No, I didn't! I didn't want to see you at all! Not you losers! It's just, when I thought I might never see your faces again, m-my chest, my chest..."

"What's this about your chest? Did it feel like it was bein' torn apart?"

"Sh-shut up, Tiny Tits!"

"Don't call them tiny!"

"I'll call 'em what I want! I'll call 'em that a million times! They're tiny, tiny, tiny, tiny, tiny, tiny, tiny, tiny, tiny, tiny, tiny, tiny, tiny, tiny, tiny, tiny, tiny, tiny, tiny, tiny, tiny, tiny, tiny, tiny, tiny, tiny!"

"Hold on," Merry grabbed Ranta by the jaw. "Shut up, and stay still. Or would you rather I not heal you?"

Merry was expressionless, her voice level. That lent her words an even greater impact.

"...N-no." Ranta sat up straight. "...I'm sorry."

"You got scolded," Yume teased.

Ranta just scowled at her, not moving an inch. He must've been awfully scared of Merry.

"...Thank...goodness..." Shihoru said, slouching to the floor.

Moguzo let out a sigh of relief, saying, "Yeah."

It suddenly occurred to Haruhiro, *We're starting to relax. It's at times like this...*

*It's at times like this when we most need to stay cautious. Our greatest enemy is mistakes brought on by letting our guards down.*

Haruhiro took note of their surroundings.

*See, they're here. They've come.*

A number of kobolds jumped out from one of the pens off in the distance.

*There are two, no, three of them? If that's all, then we can handle them, but there's no guarantee it'll stop at just three.*

"Merry, how's Ranta looking?" Haruhiro asked.

"I'm almost done with him," she said.

"Let's get out of here. Ranta, get up. You can run, right?"

"Damn straight I can! Who do think you're talking to, you trash?" Ranta snapped.

*Who're you calling trash, and how about a word of thanks, man?* Haruhiro thought.

If he'd said he hadn't thought that, it'd have been a huge lie, but Ranta was Ranta because being Ranta made Ranta Ranta. With that Yume-esque thought, he decided to just let it slide.

*Awooooooooooooooooooooooooooooooooooooooo...*

As expected, one of the kobolds howled, but Haruhiro and the others were already running away. Still, they were back to being on the run again, so the situation was still dangerous. However, it was important not to overreact.

"Head to the third level! Sorry, Merry, I'm not confident I remember the way! You lead us to the nearest well!"

"Got it!"

"Ranta, you stay next to Moguzo! Bring up the rear!"

"Got it! It pisses me off to follow orders from a loser like you, though!"

"Quit whinin'!" Yume snapped.

Yume had taken the words right out of Haruhiro's mouth, so he was able to avoid getting too angry at Ranta.

When Merry gave directions, they were precise and accurate.

A thought suddenly occurred to Haruhiro. Perhaps Merry had *wanted* to come back here. Maybe she had been going over the structure of the mines in her head, over and over, so that she could.

Merry had said she wanted to get over something.

Did she have some unfinished business or something here? Had she been secretly hoping that, someday, she'd be able to accomplish whatever that was? Was it taking revenge, like you'd expect? Or was it—

They arrived at the well. After sending the girls up first, Ranta, Moguzo, then finally Haruhiro climbed up the rope ladder.

"I'm not going to stay behind again, okay?" Ranta complained, but it wasn't that Haruhiro didn't trust him not to. He just didn't want to take any risks he didn't have to.

The kobolds didn't chase them up to the third level. After all that had happened, they were exhausted, so they decided to take a rest in a spot where there weren't so many lightflowers blooming.

Yes—that'd been the plan.

It was a dark there. Very dark. So dark they couldn't see anything. It was like a pool of darkness.

Haruhiro stopped.

"...Hold on. I heard something, a sound."

"...A sound?" Shihoru asked, cocking her head to the side.

Haruhiro listened closely.

He could hear it.

*Click, click.*

*Clack, clack.*

*Click, click.*

It was a quiet sound, but there was something moving.

*It's not a kobold—I don't think so.*

"Wait here," Ranta said, turning around and going back the way they came. He soon came back with lightflowers in his hands.

Ranta balled up two bunches of lightflowers and threw them deep into the darkness. The lightflower balls rolled up to their feet.

*—Their* feet.

"Oh! Oh...!" Moguzo cried, backing away. "...G-ghos...!"

"Eek!" Yume screamed, leapt into the air, hugged Ranta, then immediately shoved him away. "—Wha-what're you tryin' to do to me?!"

"Y-you're the one who grabbed onto me!"

"...Could they be..." Shihoru held her staff tight, her breathing quickened. "...s-skeletons...?"

"Yes." Merry stepped forward.

When she whacked the pommel of her priest's staff on the ground, there was a clear sound as the rings on it jangled.

"They're corpses given a temporary, false life by No-Life King's curse. This is what they become once they rot away. Skeletons."

"It can't be..." Haruhiro fell silent, at a loss for words.

In the area illuminated by the dim light of the lightflowers, he could see that those things—no, people—there was more than one of them.

There were three.

Each of them wore their own weapons, armor and clothing, but their exposed skin—no, there was no skin, it was bone. The slightly-yellowed white of their bones was peeking through.

One wore armor, carrying a sword. Another was dressed similarly to Haruhiro, carrying a dagger. The last wore a mage's robe, holding a staff.

"Long time no see," said Merry.

Merry was standing further forward than Haruhiro, so he couldn't see her face.

What kind of expression did Merry have now? Whatever it was, her voice wasn't wavering. She spoke in the same tone she might use to greet old friends she was seeing for the first time in ages.

Probably, she had been prepared for this.

Here in the Cyrene Mines, Merry had lost three friends. Haruhiro had never heard her say she'd come back to look for the bodies. It'd have been impossible to hold a proper service for them. She'd had no choice but to leave them here.

And those who died in the frontier lands of Grimgar—after five days at most, three at least—were turned into moving corpses by No-Life King's curse if they weren't cremated.

Merry had anticipated that her former comrades would have met that wretched end.

"Michiki. Ogu. Mutsumi." Merry called each of their names, and then said, "—I'm sorry."

"Get ready!" Haruhiro shouted.

That was because he'd seen Mutsumi, the mage, lift her staff. But, she was just bones. All that was left of her was bones, so why'd she have a voice?

"...Delm... Hel... En..." Her voice was like the sound of the wind and, honestly, it was creepy, but he didn't have time to be worrying about that.

Merry cried, "Dodge it!" and leapt to the side. Without missing a beat, Haruhiro and the rest scattered to the left and right, too.

"...Van... Arve..."

There was wind. An incredibly powerful wind blasted against him. It was no ordinary wind. It was a hot wind.

"It's hot...?!" Haruhiro reflexively covered his face with his arms.

*Still, I guess it's not hot enough to burn me. It is hot, though. It's still really hot. It feels like it'd melt my eyes out if they were open. I don't think they'll melt, though.*

"I'll use Dispel to free you from this abominable curse!" Unlike usual, it seemed like Merry meant to actively move up to the front. "I need to get closer!"

*I can't stop her,* thought Haruhiro. *Even if I tell her to stop because it's dangerous, this is one time that's not going to work. I need to let Merry do what she wants. In order to make that possible, we have to support her.*

"Moguzo, take the warrior!" he called. "Ranta, get the thief!"

With a shout, Moguzo started swinging at the warrior, Michiki.

"Leave it to me!" Likewise, Ranta sprung at the thief, Ogu.

"Yume!" Haruhiro gave Yume a signal with his eyes.

Merry was probably planning to cast Dispel on Mutsumi first. He and Yume needed to work together to lend her a hand. Yume immediately nodded and gave him a "Sure!"

"Ohhhhhhhhhh...!"

He was up against a skeleton, so it might not do much good, but Haruhiro roared as he charged straight at Mutsumi. Yume was right there with him.

*If Mutsumi shows any sign of casting, I need to dodge. That spell she used before was probably Hot Wind. It's a type of Arve Magic, I think. Arve Magic should have a lot of attack and destruction spells, so it'd be bad if we got hit by one.*

"...Delm... Hel... En..."

*Here it comes.*

Mutsumi drew elemental sigils with her staff and began to chant.

Delm, hel, en. That much was the same as before. It was Arve Magic.

"Run!"

Haruhiro darted left, while Yume let out a funny cry and threw herself to the right as hard as she could.

"...Rig... Arve..."

*What is it?*

*Something flared up. Flames.*

*It's flames. A wall of fire appeared in front of Mutsumi.*

"Firewall!" Shihoru cried in surprise, then began chanting. "Ohm, rel, ect, nemun, darsh...!"

Shihoru's spell was Shadow Bond. The shadow elemental attached itself to the ground, right in front of where Ogu was heading. Ogu stepped on it and then couldn't move anymore.

"Nice one, Shihoru!" Now that he held the advantage, Ranta redoubled his assault. "Hah, hah, hah, hah, hah...! Whuh...?!"

However, Ogu was a thief, just like Haruhiro. He used his dagger to deflect Ranta's longsword. He deflected and deflected.

It'd have been hard to do that against heavy strikes like Moguzo's, but even Haruhiro could probably have managed to deflect Ranta's attacks somehow. Ranta might not be able to defeat Ogu.

"Murgh! Hwahhhh...!"

Meanwhile, Moguzo had locked blades with Michiki. They fiercely pushed back and forth. Moguzo would've liked to use Wind to spin his sword around his opponent's, but since both of them were warriors, they each knew the other's moves, so it wasn't that simple. For now, there was no question that Moguzo was struggling.

"Wh-what can we do...?!" Yume was standing in front of the wall of fire.

*Mutsumi's on the other side. Because of the flames, we can't see her.*

"Wh-what do you mean, what—" Haruhiro's head shot back. "Ah...!!"

A small bead of light had shot through the wall, smashing Haruhiro right in the face. For a moment, he thought he was dead, but he was still perfectly alive. It hadn't done any more damage than a punch might do, but it hurt all the same.

*—Was that a Magic Missile...?!*

"Ahh!!" It sounded like Yume had been hit, too.

Beads of light were zooming around.

All Haruhiro could do was back away from the wall of fire and dodge the beads of light. He'd never realized magic could be used like this.

There was a grunt from behind him.

*Did they get Moguzo...?!*

No, it looks like he dodged it by the skin of his teeth. Michiki. That technique.

Haruhiro only saw it for an instant, but had Michiki just done a reverse somersault while swinging his blade down?

*Is that a warrior skill? So...they have those sorts of acrobatic maneuvers in their skills, too?*

Moguzo immediately tried to counterattack, but Michiki quickly jumped backwards, putting them on even footing again.

*That warrior, he's tough. Michiki. His nimble techniques are better than Moguzo's. They may be equally matched in strength, too.*

*In a one-on-one fight, eventually he's going to get the better of Moguzo. He's already starting to push him back.*

*If Moguzo gets taken down, there won't be anyone left who can hold Michiki back. We may have the numerical advantage, but if we fall one by one—we'll lose. I need to support Moguzo.*

The moment Haruhiro thought that, Shihoru cast a spell.

"Ohm, rel, ect, vel, darsh...!"

It was Shadow Beat. The shadow elemental, which looked like a black ball of seaweed, struck Michiki's shoulder. However, that was all it did. Michiki may have shaken a little, but not noticeably. Basically, that meant Shadow Beat was ineffective against skeletons.

"Shihoru, use Shadow Bond!" Haruhiro shouted.

At the exact same moment, Ranta shouted, "Your spell's worn off over here!"

When Haruhiro looked over, sure enough, Ogu was able to move freely now, and he had Ranta on the ropes.

The spell duration for Shadow Bond was supposed to be around 25 seconds. Had 25 seconds passed already? No, it didn't feel that way.

Haruhiro didn't know the details, but there were a lot of things that could make it easier or harder for a spell to work, and even when it did work, there were apparently ways to weaken the power or effect through willpower or under a number of conditions.

"I-I'm doing it now...! Ohm, rel, ect, nemun, darsh...!" Shihoru tried to catch Ogu with a Shadow Bond again, but perhaps it was too blatantly obvious. Ogu leapt over the shadow elemental on the ground, closing in on Ranta.

All the while there were beads of light shooting out from behind the wall of fire, and when they came Haruhiro had to dodge them, so—

*What am I supposed to do...?!*

"Mutsumi...!" Merry shouted her comrade's name.

"...Huh?" Haruhiro was dumbstruck by what he saw. "Wait, Merry—"

*What?*

*What in the world are you thinking?*

Merry charged towards the wall of fire.

*No way.*

*You'll get burned.*

*If you do that, you'll burn up.*

If he could have stopped her, he would've, but there was no way for him to make it in time.

Merry vanished beyond the wall of fire. "—O light! May Lumiaris' divine protection be upon you... Dispel!"

He heard Merry's voice.

Soon, the flames weakened, quickly vanishing.

Merry was crouched down on the ground.

At her feet lay a mage's robe and hat, a staff rolling on the ground. Aside from that, there was just ash.

Haruhiro tried to call out to her, but he couldn't find the words.

"I'm fine!" Merry stood up.

*How are you fine?*

*There's no way you could be fine.*

*Her hair's slightly singed. Her face's a little red from being burned, too. Of course, that's not all. Merry just struck down a comrade—someone who was probably her friend, too—and she did it with her own hands. There's no way she's fine after that.*

*But comforting her will have to wait.*

"Yume! Shihoru! Help Moguzo!" he called.

"Sure!"

"R-right..."

Having left supporting Moguzo to those two, Haruhiro tried to get behind Ogu. But, of course, his opponent was also a thief. Ogu moved around quickly, keeping Ranta in check, and never failed to keep an eye on Haruhiro so he couldn't get behind him, as well.

*He's better than me,* thought Haruhiro. Haruhiro's reflexes were nothing compared to Ogu's. *Even though he's a skeleton. His abilities must be the same as they were when he was alive.*

Probably, in a straight-up fight, Haruhiro wouldn't be able to beat Ogu. He might go down pretty easily.

*—But, sorry, Ogu. Sorry for calling you Ogu like we're pals, but me and Merry are friends, so that's why. I'm weaker than you, Ogu, but I'm not alone.*

"Ranta!" he called.

"Yeah!"

Haruhiro traded places with Ranta. At times like this, Ranta was strangely quick to pick up on what he wanted. He had good instincts.

Ogu seemed a little confused, looking like he was searching for Ranta. As if to say "You're wide open," Haruhiro thrust at Ogu.

Ogu used Swat. Next, he went for a counterattack, so this time Haruhiro used Swat. When he attacked, his opponent used Swat, when his opponent attacked, he'd use Swat.

When he used Swat for the fourth time, Haruhiro had a scare.

Ogu changed the angle of his dagger, causing Haruhiro to nearly fail to deflect it.

As he had thought, Haruhiro couldn't win against Ogu. He didn't have to.

Haruhiro stepped in, thrusting his dagger forward.

Swat was purely a technique to ward off enemy attacks, a defensive skill. So, for a moment at least, the user had to focus all of their attention on their opponent's attack. Once they got used to doing it, it became reflexive and they'd do so pretty much automatically. Perhaps even when they shouldn't.

Ogu used Swat on Haruhiro's dagger.

"There...!" At precisely that moment, Ranta came at Ogu diagonally from behind, swinging his longsword into Ogu's right leg.

Honestly, Haruhiro shuddered.

*We didn't plan that at all, so, Ranta, man, I'm amazed you knew to do that. Actually, it's creepy that you did.*

"Ogu...!"

As Ogu's leg snapped in two and he could stand no longer, Merry rushed over to him.

"O light! May Lumiaris' divine protection be upon you... Dispel!"

Was it okay for him to be watching, or should he look away? Haruhiro didn't know.

Either way, he saw Ogu engulfed in light, and the next moment his body, or rather his bones, crumble away to nothing. Haruhiro felt a pain in his chest. He even felt a little like he might cry.

Since it was Merry, who'd once been his comrade, who 'd released Ogu from his curse, he thought maybe that was a good thing. But, in another way, he felt it wasn't good at all. It was too cruel for Merry.

Merry fell to her knees, scooping up the ashes that had once been Ogu in her hands. Even as she grasped at them, they slipped through her fingers.

Merry looked down, hanging her head. "...Now it's just Michiki."

"Hey!" It wasn't clear what Ranta was thinking, but he leveled his longsword at Merry. "You've got us with you now! Don't you forget it!"

No, Haruhiro did kind of get what he was trying to say. But there were probably more polite, or more accurate, ways to put it, and what was he pointing a sword at her for?

Well, regardless, Merry lifted her face, saying, "Yeah." She even had a smile as she did so, so maybe it was okay.

"Haruhiro-kun!" Shihoru shouted.

"We're doing this!" Haruhiro turned back to face Michiki.

Michiki was slowly driving Moguzo into a corner. It looked like neither Yume or Shihoru could do much about it. If Moguzo stepped on a Shadow Bond, that'd be a disaster, so maybe it was difficult.

"Ranta's on the scene!" Ranta took a swing at Michiki from his flank.

Michiki easily turned the blow away with his sword, but it let Moguzo, who had been in a pretty bad spot, catch a breath.

Haruhiro decided to target Michiki's back.

*Michiki's more observant than Moguzo, but he's no Ogu. Ranta keeps on attacking without hesitation, and Moguzo can be pretty skillful, and he's good at working in sync with his comrades. We can do this.*

*—Here.*

*Now's the time.*

Haruhiro grappled Michiki from behind. He was all bones, so

poking and stabbing him with the dagger wasn't going to do any good.

He took him by the neck. Wrapping both arms around it, he tore Michiki's skull off of his spinal column. Right after that, Moguzo's bastard sword slammed into Michiki's right arm.

"Hungh...!"

Michiki's right hand and sword sailed through the air.

"—O light! May Lumiaris' divine protection be upon you..."

Merry was coming.

She brought her five fingers to her forehead, making a pentagram. Then, pressing her middle finger to her brow, she completed the symbol of Lumiaris, the hexagram.

Merry pointed the palm of her hand towards Michiki. "Dispel...!"

The light was brilliant, yet somehow felt sad. Michiki crumbled away in Haruhiro's arms.

*The way only the things he was carrying and his ashes are left behind, it's just too cruel.*

*Though, it was the same for Manato. It's the same for everyone. When you die, this is what happens. In the end, this is what dying is.*

When the light faded away, Haruhiro slumped to the ground. He couldn't say anything. He couldn't think anything. Nothing came to his mind.

Merry crouched down in front of what had once been Michiki. Moguzo and Ranta stood still. Yume, too. Shihoru held her hat, her shoulders heaving with labored breaths.

"...We've cleared them out," Ranta said.

"We have," Merry said, scooping up Michiki's ashes and closing her eyes. "—It's over. Finally, it's done. I've done what I had to. I couldn't have done it without all of you. Thank you."

"He was strong," Moguzo said, sighing. "He was strong, that Michiki guy. I need to get stronger, too."

Shihoru nodded her head, "...I want more firepower. I want to learn new spells. I have to..."

"Hmm," Ranta held his chin pensively. "Maybe I'll develop my own super attack, one that's good enough to suit me."

*There he goes, saying stupid stuff again. He gets ignored.*

"Yume wants to try raisin' a wolf dog," Yume said. "For one gold, they'll let her have a puppy. It sounds like it takes a long time for them to grow up, though."

"...What will you do with it until then?" Haruhiro tried asking, just to see her response.

Yume tilted her head to the side. "It won't grow attached if it's not with Yume, so maybe she'll have to try puttin' it in her pocket and carryin' it around like that, huh."

"Will it fit? In a pocket...?" Merry asked.

Yume touched her front pocket. "Mmm, dunno. Maybe it'd have a liiiiittle bit of a hard time fittin'. Maybe Yume should buy a bag for carryin' it."

Ranta, despite being Ranta, and, because he was Ranta, having no right to be, was taken aback. "...Listen, that's going to be really heavy."

"Yume's the one who'll be carryin' it, so it's fine. Ah, just sayin' this now, but Yume's neeeever lettin' you touch it, Ranta."

"Why not?" he objected. "You could let me pet it, at least. If I pet it, it's sure to grow up strong."

"It will not!"

"Will too!"

"Will! Not!"

"It will!"

"Nuh-uh, no way!"

"It'd get so strong, you dolt!"

"There's this saying about not counting your chickens..." Haruhiro said with a wry laugh, then sighed. "Oh, whatever."

*We have to get stronger, huh.*

Getting stronger.

What would that mean for Haruhiro?

He'd gained a number of skills, but he didn't think he could become dramatically stronger that way. No matter how much he polished his Backstab and Spider, they had limits. It was important to build his own strength, too, but maybe by growing as a leader, he could lift the power of the group as a whole. That said, it probably wouldn't be an obvious, perceptible improvement.

In the end, maybe a plainer role just suited Haruhiro.

"Merry," he said.

"What?"

"Are you good? You don't want to, you know...bring back a memento, or something?"

"Ah," Merry's eyes widened a little, as if caught by surprise. "It hadn't occurred to me. Let's see. Yes, I'll bring something back. When we get back to Alterna, I'll have to tell Hayashi, too."

"Yeah. You should. I'm sure Hayashi-san will be relieved to hear it."

"I hope so."

Merry started going through the equipment Michiki had left behind. Haruhiro came close to suggesting she heal their wounds, but thought better of it. Merry was lovingly checking over the things Michiki, Ogu and Mutsumi had left behind. He felt like it'd be wrong to disturb her.

"...Today has been exhausting," Shihoru mumbled.

Yume gently swung both her arms in circles, saying, "You got that right."

"It's not over yet," Haruhiro said, cautioning them sternly. "We shouldn't take it easy until we're back in Alterna. Well, I don't think we should run into anything else, though."

"I wouldn't be so sure," Ranta said, smirking.

*Stop it. Don't be like that. When you say things like that, that's how we get into situations like this.*

A shudder ran down his spine.

Haruhiro turned around.

"—Dea..."

"Huh?" Ranta turned around, too. "Oh..."

Moguzo said, "This is bad."

"Huh?" Yume said, her head in the clouds.

Shihoru let out a short, little shriek.

"No way..." Merry said, the words slipping out without her intending them to.

*Why?*

*Why now, of all times?*

It would have been trouble at any time, but this was just too much.

"Run—" That was all Haruhiro managed to say.

*It's here. It's coming. It's really coming. Seriously? Please, stop. What's going on? Why?*

It had black and white spotted fur, a massive body that was almost too big to belong to a kobold, and in its hands, it held a thick, and much too large, carving knife.

Death Spots.

Death Spots panted wildly, its saliva dripping and splattering everywhere as it charged at them, a harsh glint in its two blood-red eyes.

It had three minions that looked like elders following it, each of them wearing armor and helmets and carrying swords and round shields.

*This is no good. There's no way we can win this,* Haruhiro thought wildly.

*But, what if we turn to run? No, that's no good either.*

*If we show our backs, they'll kill us all in no time.*

*I don't want to fight them, but we have to. If we're going to fight them, I can't think about losing.*

*We have to win. What can we do to win?*

"Sorry, Moguzo, you take Death Spots!" Haruhiro shouted. "Everyone else will handle the others!"

He couldn't hear everyone's responses. Haruhiro was panicking. Could anyone blame him? For now, they had to take out the minions as quickly as possible. Everything started with that.

"Ohm, rel, ect, nemun, darsh...!" Shihoru fired off a Shadow Bond spell, stopping one minion in its tracks. Thanks to that, Haruhiro calmed down just a little.

"Ranta, you take one...! Yume and I will take the other...!"

"I've got this!"

"Nyaa!"

"I'll go, too!" Merry came with Haruhiro and Yume, priest's staff in hand. Haruhiro was about to stop her, but then reconsidered.

*Until we kill the minions, maybe I should have Merry come up front* with us. *Once the minions are taken down, I'll have her back off. Yeah. Let's go with that.*

"Thanks...!" Moguzo put all his might into a Thanks Slash, but Death Spots easily knocked it away using its carving knife. Then it immediately went on the counterattack. It was an angry torrent of blows, the carving knife striking at Moguzo.

Shouting each time, Moguzo was somehow managing to stop the hits, but—if he failed, even once, it looked like the blow would be fatal, even through his armor.

Haruhiro was scared, but it must have been even scarier for Moguzo.

*He's resisting his terror to block the blows. Somehow, we need to make use of the time. No, not "somehow." We're definitely going to do it.*

The two minions ignored Death Spots fighting with Moguzo and rushed onwards towards Haruhiro and the others.

"Hatred...!" Ranta sprung towards Minion C, causing it to falter.

"I'll do it!" Haruhiro ran past Yume, charging at Minion B. Even so, he didn't mean to attack it.

Minion B swung its sword.

Swat.

He deflected it with his dagger.

As he deflected and deflected and deflected, Yume and Merry moved around to Minion B's sides to flank it.

"Diagonal Cross!"

"Smash!"

Yume and Merry attacked simultaneously from both sides. Minion B blocked with its sword and shield, but its stance was broken.

*Now.* Haruhiro got behind Minion B, then used Spider.

Grappling it from behind, he raised the face guard on its helmet then jabbed his dagger into its right eye. He twisted, pulled it out, and jumped away.

Minion B was still breathing, so Merry gave it a punishing blow with her priest's staff and Yume kicked it to the ground with a shout.

Minion B wasn't getting back up. Two more to go.

Should he go for Minion A, which was held in place by Shadow Bond, or Minion C, which Ranta was handling?

Haruhiro headed for Minion A without hesitation. Yume and Merry came with him. Minion A couldn't move, so it would be easy.

With Yume and Merry drawing its attention, Haruhiro circled around behind it. Spider. He finished it off with the same process as Minion B, then headed on to Minion C.

*But, what about Moguzo? He looks like he's having a really hard time. Just now, when he blocked the carving knife with his bastard sword, it looked like his knees were going to buckle. He managed to recover, but—he can't hold out on his own like that anymore.*

"I can handle this guy alone!" Ranta shouted.

Haruhiro didn't hesitate. "—I'm counting on you!"

*I'll believe. In my comrades.*

"Merry, stand back!" Haruhiro ordered. Yume and him took up positions to the side and behind Death Spots to put pressure on it. But, rather than them putting pressure on it...

*What is this? Why does it feel so intimidating?*

Death Spots had its back to Haruhiro. It wasn't even sparing a glance in his direction. Despite that, he had no idea how to even go about attacking. No matter how he attacked, he had the feeling it would be useless.

Whether it was useless or not, he had to do it.

That's right. He had to.

Haruhiro tried to go for a Backstab. That was the plan. However, the next thing he knew, he was laid out flat on the ground.

*What?*

*Maybe, when I tried to close in from behind, Death Spots kicked me, or something?*

*It's hazy, but I have some recollection of that happening. Is my body all right?* Haruhiro got up. *It hurts here and there, and I feel a bit dizzy. I don't really know for sure, but I'm probably fine.*

"Take that, and that, and that, and that, and that...!" Ranta shouted, knocking away Minion C's sword and shield with a combo attack that went faster than the eye could follow. It looked so forced, but it looked like he was getting results with it.

Ranta knocked Minion C's helmet away with the tip of his blade, then buried his longsword deep in its throat. "—Wahaha! One vice...!"

*Even at a time like this, it's the vice he cares about? I have to question his humanity, but he's reliable nonetheless.*

"Now it's just Death Spots!" Haruhiro said boldly, loud enough that everyone could hear. He wanted to encourage the others as much as he could.

Though, he also doubted he could.

Death Spots was howling "Awoogahahaha! Awoogahahaha! Awoogahahahahah!" as it completely overwhelmed Moguzo.

Haruhiro, Yume, and even Ranta wanted to help Moguzo, of course. But they couldn't get close enough.

*Why not? Is it this intimidating aura? Is something as vague and undefined as that the reason?*

*No.*

It was Death Spots' movements. They were insanely dynamic, making it seem almost as if its legs were spring-loaded as it bounded around swinging its knife-sword. Death Spots never stopped moving. Because of that, they couldn't focus on a target.

*Still, it has to have habits and patterns it follows, right? If I could just learn those...*

*No, I don't have time to take it easy like that.*

"Ohm, rel, ect, vel, darsh...!" Shihoru cast Shadow Beat.

*Her timing seemed perfect, but no luck, huh?*

Death Spots swung its knife-sword with a bark, easily slashing the black seaweed-like mass of the shadow elemental and causing it to vanish.

However, for an instant, that created an opening, though hardly one that deserved to be called an opening.

"Guh...!"

Moguzo, who had been on the defensive all this time, went on the offensive.

He was already starting to get winded, and he must have taken some wounds, too, but if he let Death Spots wail on him for much longer, he was guaranteed to have his defense broken. He had no choice but to take a big risk. That was what Moguzo must have decided. Haruhiro didn't think he was wrong. It was clearly the only option. But, even if he did...

"Gwoohahah...!"

Death Spots knocked away Moguzo's bastard sword, not with its knife-sword but, incredibly, with its left arm.

*What the hell was that? How is that fair?*

Haruhiro was dumbstruck, but that must have been nothing compared to the shock Moguzo had felt. Actually, even if he hadn't been shocked by it at all, the result would have been the same.

With a "Gwahahh...!" Death Spots slammed its knife-sword into Moguzo's left shoulder. The knife-sword tore through his armor, sinking in much deeper than his collarbone.

"Moguzooooo...!" Ranta leapt at Death Spots.

*You're crazy. That's way too reckless.*

Ranta was nearly cut in two by Death Spots' return swing, but he shrieked and ducked down, having it miss him by a hair.

*Still, that was nice. Thanks to that, Moguzo was able to roll away from Death Spots. Though he's bleeding pretty heavily and it looks like a serious wound.*

"Merry, go to Moguzo...!" Haruhiro needn't have said anything. Merry was already trying to heal Moguzo.

*Time. I have to buy her time.*

At some point, Yume had readied her bow and arrow. "There!" she fired. From relatively close up.

She hit. It struck Death Spots in the flank. Death Spots howled in anger, turning to face Yume.

"Don't you look away from me...!" Ranta attacked. But Death Spots easily deflected Ranta's longsword with its knife-sword, launching a fierce assault on Yume.

Yume, of course, ran away. "Scary, scary, scary...!"

She ditched her bow, using her Pit Rat skill to roll around trying to get away.

Haruhiro was chasing after Death Spots, but he couldn't do anything. Or rather, he couldn't even keep up with Death Spots.

"—Dammit!" he shouted.

"O darkness, O Lord of Vice...!" Ranta chanted a spell. "Demon Call...!"

From who knows where, something that looked like a blackish purple human torso with no head appeared. It had two hole-like eyes and beneath them, a gash-like mouth. It was the demon Zodiac-kun.

"Now go, Zodiac-kun!" he bellowed.

"...Don't wanna... No way... *Keehehehe... Keehehehehehe... Eehehehehehe...*"

"Tch, yeah, didn't think that'd fly..."

*...The hell are you doing, man? This is an emergency.* Haruhiro was too disgusted for words. Not that he had time for talking right now.

"Agh...!" Yume got kicked by Death Spots and sent flying.

"Argh! C'mere, you...!" Ranta grabbed Zodiac-kun by the arm and dragged the demon with him.

*He's able to do stuff like that, too?*

Then Ranta chucked Zodiac-kun at Death Spots. "Taaaaake thiiiiis...!"

(...Curse you... Curse you, curse you, curse youuuuuuuuuuuuuuuuu...)

Zodiac-kun collided with Death Spots—or rather, ended up clinging to its face. Death Spots pulled the demon off and threw it away in short order, but during that time, Ranta had been closing in. "Anger...!"

He went for the neck. But Death Spots twisted out of the way, meaning that Ranta's outthrust longsword only shaved a few centimeters off of its neck, fur included. That said, it was still a hit. Blood didn't spurt out, but there was some bleeding.

*Nice,* thought Haruhiro. *This isn't an enemy that's going to be undefeatable no matter what we do. We can do this. If we do it right, we can fight this guy. We might even be able to win.*

He only felt that way for a brief moment.

"Fshrrruuuuuuuuuuuuuuuuuu...!" The color of Death Spots' eyes changed. It had a shine in its eyes that was completely different from before.

"—Gwah...!"

Ranta was pulverized in an instant.

*But, just now—what happened?*

Haruhiro hadn't been able to see it.

*Whatever it was, it left Ranta knocked down and bloody. Death Spots is lifting that knife-sword aloft—is it planning to finish off Ranta?*

*There's something clinging to its sword arm. It's blackish purple and—*Haruhiro's eyes went wide.

"Zodiac-kun...?!"

"Keehehehe... Keehehehehehehe... Eekekekekekeke... Keehehehehehe-hehehe...!"

With a bark, Death Spots grabbed Zodiac-kun and, as if to say *You're in the way,* it slammed the demon against the ground. Zodiac-kun vanished with a hiss, as if evaporating. But thanks to the demon, Ranta survived.

Death Spots swung its knife-sword down at Ranta. As it did, Moguzo jumped in, groaning in exertion as he stopped the blow with his bastard sword.

*If Zodiac-kun hadn't been there, or hadn't interfered with Death Spots, what would've happened? Probably, Moguzo wouldn't have made it. Zodiac-kun saved Ranta.*

Shihoru had just finished helping Yume to her feet, but Yume was still holding her gut. It looked like she was in a lot of pain.

Even as Moguzo was pushed around by Death Spots, he was trying to get it away from Ranta, who had fallen and couldn't move.

"Death Spots gets stronger the more wounded it is!" Merry shouted, rushing over to Ranta. "—Haru! I'm going to run out of magic soon! Two more times, three if I push it, that's my limit!"

Haruhiro inhaled sharply and gritted his teeth.

*Moguzo... Even with Merry healing his wounds, it doesn't restore his stamina. He's already gasping for breath.*

*The more we hurt it, the stronger it gets? The more we manage to drive it into a corner, the harder it'll be on us, who are already cornered? What the hell is that? What do we even do about it?*

*There's nothing to do.*

*We run.*

*That's all we can do.*

*But can we run? If we could get away, we'd have done that to begin with. No, back then it had three minions, so the situation's changed. Now it's just Death Spots. Still, can all of us run away safely?*

*Death Spots is fast. If it gives chase, there's pretty much no doubt that it'll catch us. If it attacked us from behind, we wouldn't stand a chance. It'd only take an instant for it to kill one of us. If one person dies instantly, it'll get a second, then a third—No, it's no good. We all run together. That's what I want to do, but it's not realistic. We'd have to sacrifice a few of us, and even if we got away, it'd be a few of us at best. At worst, we'd all be wiped out.*

*One person. At a minimum, one person needs to stay behind. One person will delay Death Spots. Literally by putting their life on the line.*

*That one person will die. If one person dies, the other five can live.*

*It's the only option. I know that. We'll do it. While I'm agonizing over it, Moguzo could get taken down. If that happens, we're finished. It'll be a rout. Everyone will die. We'll be wiped out. I can't let that happen.*

*I have to kill one person. In order to save five. But, who will it be? Who's going to delay it? Do I have to say that to them? "Everyone's going to run, so take care of that thing while we do. Please, die." To, say, Moguzo, for instance?*

"—Okay!" Ranta jumped to his feet. It looked like he was healed.

Haruhiro closed his eyes. "...I'm sorry, everyone."

*For being such a pathetic leader.*

*Still, I can't do what I can't do.*

Haruhiro grappled Death Spots from behind as it tried to beat Moguzo into the ground. He managed it surprisingly easily, though not enough to be disappointingly so.

*Because I've already resolved myself, and I don't feel fear anymore, is that it? Doesn't matter.*

Death Spots tried to shake off Haruhiro.

*I won't let you do that. I'm not letting go.*

Clinging on desperately, Haruhiro pounded Death Spots in the head with the pommel of his dagger. He hit it again, and again. As he did, he shouted, "Moguzo, Ranta! Merry, Yume, Shihoru! Now's your chance! Run away!"

"B-B-but...!" someone said, Moguzo he thought, but he wasn't sure.

"Just do it...!" Haruhiro was frantic. He whacked it with the dagger. Over and over.

Death Spots was still a kobold and its body structure made it even less able to reach its arms around behind its back than a human. Still, it was managing to strike Haruhiro with its elbows or something. It didn't seem like it would be able to slice him with the knife-sword, but it was able to hit Haruhiro in the back and in the head.

*Oh, crap. I feel like I'm about to start whimpering. I feel like I'm going to lose my grip before I can start whimpering. I won't lose my grip, though.*

"—Are you going to make my death be in vain?!" he shouted. "I'm not going to make it! Look how beat up I am! I'm done! Please, run! Come on, I'm begging you!"

"Let's go!" Ranta shouted.

*Oh, Ranta.*

*That's good, you being like that. There's the Ranta I know. We'd be in real trouble without you in the party. Keep on dragging everyone along with you that way. It's something only you can do. I'm counting on you.*

For a moment, Haruhiro saw Yume looking in his direction. But Yume's body was facing the other way—she'd just turned her head back to look. She was getting ready to go. He felt relieved. If Yume would run, he was sure Shihoru would, too.

*Yume, when you patted my head, I thought, "Oh, this is nice." Shihoru, don't drag your memories of Manato with you for too long.*

"Haru!" Merry shouted his name.

*Go. Please, go. You know, I think I'd started to like you, and I want you to live on, Merry, so, please, just go.*

He could hear Moguzo roar, his voice fading into the distance.

*That's good,* thought Haruhiro. *Run, Moguzo. You're strong. You've definitely been getting stronger. You'll get even stronger still. Moguzo, you're the core of the party. We're all dependent on you, you could say.*

*But, it's not "we" anymore, huh.*

*Because I won't be part of the group anymore.*

*I'm all alone now.*

*Not that there was any helping it. I made the choice myself.*

*I couldn't have made any other choice. I could never have asked one of you to die for me. If I was going to have to do that, I figured I'd rather die myself.*

*I'm sure this must be hard on all of you. You don't want to sacrifice me to survive, do you? I don't want you to think of it that way, but you will, won't you?*

*Still, I want you to overcome it. I dunno how to say this, but unless you overcome it, it won't have been worth me pulling this stupid stunt.*

*Michiki. Ogu. Mutsumi.*

*If I die here, will I end up like you did?*

*If I do, I hope Merry will cast Dispel on me. Please, turn me to ashes. Once that happens, just maybe, will someone join the party and take my place?*

*You know, somehow...that makes me feel incredibly lonely, and sad. I wish I hadn't imagined that. Though, maybe, I was just at my limit.*

Haruhiro felt his body floating in the air.

*Uh oh.*

He'd let go.

He'd let go of Death Spots.

He fell to the ground. Death Spots was getting ready to run. Wasn't he going to kill Haruhiro? Did he plan to leave the half-dead Haruhiro behind and chase down the rest of the party?

*No. No, no, no, no, no, no.*

How much time had Haruhiro bought them? How far had his

comrades run? It felt to him like a long time had passed. But, maybe it wasn't actually that long? He couldn't tell.

"Hey...!"

Haruhiro rose up. Death Spots didn't turn around.

*I won't let you go. Did you think I would?*

*Don't be ridiculous.*

—At that moment, he saw the line.

It wasn't blurry, Haruhiro saw a line of light, plain as day, and he moved.

*I'm slow,* he thought. *Why am I so slow? But it's not just me, Death Spots is slow, too. Well, I guess that's fine, then.*

*I managed to catch up and all.*

*Is this the spot? On Death Spots' back? There must be an internal organ or something here, huh?*

He leapt onto the kobold, stabbing his dagger in there. It slid in smoothly, reaching the spot.

Haruhiro didn't doubt it for a moment. This was the end.

Death Spots tripped, falling down where it was.

For some time, Haruhiro buried his face in Death Spots' filthy fur, but eventually he rolled over on to his side.

When he tried to speak, a strange *ohhh* sound leaked out from the back of his throat. When he tried touching his face and neck, it was all a mess of blood. There was pain, too. It then crossed his mind, *What'll I do if they leave me behind like this? I'd really rather not have that happen. Though, I don't think I can move.*

"Heyyyyy..." Haruhiro managed to raise his voice and call for his comrades.

He believed they would come for him.

He was right.

## 17. A Lie and Yesterday, Today and Tomorrow

"Yo, Harucchi! I heard, I heard, taking down Death Spots is, like, super cool! I might just get jealous of you myself! Yay, jealousy!"

While they were drinking at Sherry's Tavern, Kikkawa came over, as noisy and irritating as ever. Thanks to all of Ranta's bragging, it was widely known that Haruhiro and his group had taken down *the* Death Spots.

*Well, not that I mind,* Haruhiro thought. *Even if we just got lucky, it's true we took down Death Spots, and it feels better than being called the Goblin Slayers forever.*

"Ahhh. Still, thank goodness," Yume rested her head in her arms at the table, sighing. "Honestly, Yume kept on thinkin' we might be done for."

"Y-yeah," said Moguzo, sounding a little sleepy. "It was really dangerous..."

Shihoru looked resentfully at Haruhiro "...And a certain *someone* had to do something crazy."

"No, that was, you know..." Haruhiro scratched his head, then coughed to clear his throat. "—Yeah. I'm reflecting on my actions. I'm sorry."

"Huh...?" Shihoru looked down, awkwardly. "I-it was a joke. I wasn't blaming you or anything. Really, I mean it..."

Yume hummed pensively, "If Haru-kun hadn't stopped Tetrapods, Yume and everyone might've met our mutual disruption."

"...Yume. It's mutual destruction, okay? Not mutual disruption." Haruhiro had to correct her.

Yume cocked her head to the side quizzically. "Huh? Mutual deathtruction?"

"No, wrong. Not death, des. Also, it's not Tetrapods, it's Death Spots."

"Oh. Is it? It's all so confusin'."

"B-b-but, still!" Moguzo said, pointing to the knife-sword he had at his side. "It all worked out well in the end. All's well that ends well, they say..."

"That's right, huh. Moguzo, you ended up gettin' yourself a new weapon and all."

"Yeah..." Shihoru nodded. "That bastard sword was getting pretty beaten up..."

"I-it was, wasn't it?" Moguzo had a big grin on his face. "What should I do? About a name for this sword. I've been wondering what I should call it. I can't come up with anything..."

Yume offered "Carving Knife-kun #1" as a suggestion, but Shihoru reservedly objected.

*It seems like Moguzo wants to give it a cool name, but what's cool, I wonder? External Blaze Executioner, or something like that?*

Haruhiro decided not to say the name he'd come up with. *No matter what, that one's just too awful. Isn't there anything good?*

Ranta was off making merry with Kikkawa. Both of them were telling the other volunteer soldiers stories of their exploits with Death Spots. Somehow, they were making it sound like Kikkawa had been there, too, and Haruhiro wasn't sure if he was okay with that or not.

A little earlier, Merry had said she was going to speak to Hayashi and had gone up to the second level. Maybe this would help her come to terms with things a little.

Haruhiro took a sip of beer, frowning a bit. *It's bitter.*

*I'm glad no one had to die. I'm relieved that I survived. Still, I can't be happy from the bottom of my heart. Was it okay like that? Didn't I make a mistake? Wasn't there a better way, a better option I could have chosen? At the time, I thought it was the best I could do.*

*Right now, if I found myself in the same situation, I feel like I'd end up doing the same thing again. But is that really okay? Wasn't there some measure I could have taken before we ended up in that desperate situation?*

*With nothing but regrets coming to mind, I can't really be happy. It doesn't seem that way for everyone else, though. Why is that? Why is it just me?*

Haruhiro was the leader, and that made him different from the rest of his comrades.

*Is that why? There's a gap there. Is there any way to fill it? Are things always going to be like this...?*

"What's up?" someone asked, tapping him on the shoulder. When he looked, it was Merry. She was pretty close, which startled him a bit.

"...Ah. You're back?"

"Yeah. I am now. Did something happen?" she asked.

"Wh-why?" he stammered.

"You were acting a little strange."

"Really? I don't think I was. There's nothing much...really."

Merry smiled slightly. "You're a bad liar, Haru."

"...Am I?" Haruhiro slid his chair over a bit and Merry sat in the seat next to him.

Yume, Shihoru and Moguzo were still passionately debating what the knife-sword's name should be.

*I found myself wanting to talk to Merry. A few days ago, I might've opened up to her about my worries, but I won't do that anymore. Probably, it's because I've developed an awareness of my position. Whether or not I have the ability, or the aptitude—I'm the party's leader, aren't I? If I don't keep myself together, everyone will die.*

"Really, it's nothing." Haruhiro said, then smiled and added, "Well, that's a lie, but I'm not lying."

Merry put her hand on Haruhiro's shoulder again. Merry's soft hand didn't linger long, but it was enough to make Haruhiro feel rewarded for his efforts.

*I won't laugh at myself for being simple and easily pleased. When something makes you happy, it's okay to be happy. Because the good time won't last forever. They might end at any time.*

"Hey, Haruhiro!" Ranta and Kikkawa had their arms around each other's shoulders and came skipping over to him. "The rest of you guys, too! C'mere for a bit! Kemuri from the Day Breakers just happens to be here for a drink, and he wants to treat us to a round for taking down Death Spots!"

"You may never get another ce-chan like this, Harucchi! Ce-chan-ce-chan!"

"...What's a ce-chan supposed to be?" Haruhiro shrugged his shoulders and sighed, then blinked a few times. "Huh? Wait, the Day Breakers? You mean Souma's group?"

"Ohhh," Yume's eyes went wide.

"...Somehow, this has turned into a big deal..." Shihoru shrunk into herself.

Moguzo kept standing up and sitting down, saying, "Wh-wh-wh-what should we do?"

"It's a kind offer," Merry said, looking unfazed. "So why don't we go?"

Haruhiro was a bit surprised to find himself immediately nodding. Up until yesterday, regardless of what the final decision had been, he would've started by hesitating. What was different between the him of yesterday and the him of today? What would the him of tomorrow be like?

If he didn't die today, he'd get to meet the him of tomorrow. Just perhaps, that might be a wonderful thing.

"Let's go, everyone," he said.